A SHEEPISH ENCOUNTER AT PEMBERLEY

A PRIDE AND PREJUDICE VARIATION

BELLA BREEN

BREEN PUBLISHING

For my friends that supported me over the last horrible year: Vash, Lisa H., Brenda B., Leela, Samantha, Emma, Liz S., my sister Kathleen Curran and most especially to Kate McKeever who is the wind beneath my wings and without whom I would not have made it through the year.

Tremendous thanks goes to Elizabeth Ann West who without her amazing assistance this book would not have gotten published.

And especially to my family members that died in the last year: my dad, followed by Sandcat my feral cat I rescued and tamed, followed by my beloved corgi Munchkin.

CHAPTER 1

*I*t is a truth universally acknowledged that a sheep farmer in possession of a flock must be in want of a buyer.

The sheep, all prodigiously woolly and baaing at a loud volume, scattered across Mr. Darcy's fields, the drive, and onto the grounds of his ancestral home while he watched from the back of his horse.

"Move along!" Mr. Wentworth, his steward, was waving his hat and pushing the sheep farmer to herd the flock in the right direction. Namely off the lane and estate of Pemberley.

Mr. Darcy would not be surprised if the damnable contrary animals did not next stampede straight for the lake in front of his home. That was the only consistent action he had perceived from the beasts' behavior. They would see the possibility of making his life more troublesome and immediately pursue it.

"Johnny, bring the dog over here. Get those sheep out of the fields!" yelled the sheepherder, one of Mr. Darcy's tenants.

The tenant's son was ten years of age and old enough to help with taking the sheep to the market in Lambton. Unfortunately, Johnny was small for his age and could not see over the mounds of wool on the sheep. And their herding dog was also too short or muddled to be of much aid in the matter.

Mr. Darcy was trapped, unable to proceed down his long drive to his home or even ride over the grounds. The sheep were everywhere and immovable, as only woolly sheep could be. He had galloped from London to arrive a day early before the rest of his friends. A hot bath and good supper were all he had yearned for the last ten miles.

His horse was neither enjoying the noises nor the bleating beasts rubbing against his legs. Their greasy wool affronted his nose with a stench he hoped to never endure again. It was a miracle the wool ever ended up as crisp white yarn at all.

But Fitzwilliam Darcy knew his riches were due to generations of sheep farmers, so he did not grumble the wait. Not until his horse's patience ran out at being so near his stall and not making any progress. His horse reared up repeatedly and attempted to step sideways but was wedged by ewes on all sides. When Caesar gathered himself to rear up once more, Mr. Darcy knew it was time to find an alternate route home. Lest he be forcefully removed from his horse's back.

Mr. Darcy guided Caesar towards a sparser portion of the flock. He encouraged his horse forward through the dense gathering. Caesar knew the way home, but his eagerness to get to the rubdown and oats awaiting was no rival to the stubborn nature of Derbyshire sheep. Especially those laden down with wool.

The advance was slow. Caesar thrust against the sheep in front of him, causing them to baa louder. Caesar's ears were pinned back, and Mr. Darcy fortified himself as well as he could for a biting and kicking horse. The unending baaing had given him a dreadful headache. He was optimistic they could have made faster progress in winter. In a blizzard. On foot.

He sighed as his horse stepped forward. The number of times they had marched against the tide in the last several minutes could be counted on one hand. After what seemed like hours, he could observe, at last, the final curve in his driveway. But the lane resembled a sheepwalk. He would ask his steward what had caused this debacle after he had supper and a bath. Mr. Darcy would not disturb the sheepherder attempting to round up the mischievous livestock.

Mr. Darcy nudged his horse towards the left of the lake, which had fewer sheep, but Caesar refused and yanked to the right instead. This was not a development he had expected, as his horse was usually a docile and obedient gelding. But he understood why, as going around the lake to the right was the shorter distance to the stable yard.

With a click of teeth, he pulled the rein to the left. "Come, Caesar. We will arrive much quicker if we go this way and avoid the larger grouping."

He was grateful his friends had not traveled with him. Mr. Darcy had departed London a day early to prepare for his sister Georgiana, Mr. Bingley, the Hursts, and Miss Bingley. It was lucky they had not accompanied him into this muddle.

Even though Caesar had flicked an ear back, the horse refused to move, neither moving to the right nor left. Mr. Darcy sighed and dismounted, hauling the reins over the horse's head. He would have to lead his horse the rest of the distance. Hopefully, once they reached the lake, he could mount up. He did not want to arrive, leading his horse as if he had tumbled and could not get up again. The news would fly around Derbyshire before he would have finished his bath.

It had been a long day, and thoughts of final preparations before his guests arrived filled his mind. They had tramped past almost the entire side of the lake and were near a copse of trees. He saw a flash of white before he was hit in the legs! Knocked down, Mr. Darcy landed on his side and rolled. Frantically he grabbed at the lawn but failed to stop before landing with a large splash in the cold lake.

Gasping, he pushed up from the muddy bottom and stood. Wiping the sopping wet hair out of his eyes, he glared at the sheep staring at him from the bank. Caesar was nowhere in sight and most likely had dashed straight to the stable. He sighed again. At least no one had seen his disgraceful fall. But he did not place good odds on entering Pemberley without a servant noticing him. "Damnable, cursed creatures!"

Mr. Darcy struggled to pull his boot out of the mud. His progression toward the nearest bank was quite slow. His waterlogged clothing was heavy, and he kept sliding in the muck. After just a few steps, he slipped and fell, landing face-first in the shallows of the lake. He heaved himself out of the lake again, sputtering and pulling at his cravat.

His valet would have an apoplectic fit at the state of his clothing. None were fit to be worn again. Yanking his cravat off, he hurled it toward the bank, followed by his jacket and waistcoat. His shirt was half out of his breeches, but it did not matter. No one but a servant would see him in such a state, most likely a stable lad jogging to determine what had happened to Caesar's rider.

Mr. Darcy stumbled slowly, determined not to slip and fall again, towards the bank nearest Pemberley.

Finally out of the lake, he cautiously walked up the bank towards a copse of trees, his boots squelching. Thank goodness he had seen no visitor's carriages parked at the front steps. That would have been too much of a blow to his pride.

CHAPTER 2

*M*rs. Reynolds, the elderly housekeeper who had served the Darcy family for a generation, pointed out, "...and there's a fine prospect from that window down towards the lake."

Elizabeth Bennet ambled to the window, gazing out but not seeing, as amazement at the grandeur and magnitude of Pemberley humbled her.

"Look at this, my dear!" exclaimed Mrs. Gardiner from across the music room.

Mr. Gardiner responded, "Oh, it's quite magnificent."

Her gaze roved the terrace and the lake that was pleasingly situated. "Of all this," she whispered, "I might have been mistress."

"This piano has just arrived. It is a present from my master for Miss Georgiana."

"Your master is away, we understand," stated Mr. Gardiner.

"Yes, but we expect him here tomorrow, sir." Elizabeth swiveled towards the housekeeper, her heart pounding. "He is coming with a large party of friends," continued the housekeeper.

She spun away, clutching her reticule, almost dizzy with relief. Only a day, a scant four and twenty hours had rescued her from humiliation.

Mrs. Gardiner gestured for her niece to join them. The trio marched out the doors onto the terrace encompassing Pemberley's entire side. They were all hushed. Elizabeth mulled over her insignificance compared to the residents of this stately, grand estate. She descended the stairs, her aunt needing to rest before taking a tour of the grounds.

Elizabeth strode down a slight hill towards the small lake, peering over her shoulder for any carriages appearing. She still felt she was trespassing and feared the arrival at any second by a grim and incensed Mr. Darcy. In her mind, he wore the same expression she had last seen on the grounds of Rosings Park. She was still humiliated at how sharply she had rejected him since she had been terribly wrong about Mr. Wickham.

But she had not forgotten that he had deserved her rage over his machinations with Jane and Mr. Bingley. And she would not forget that, particularly now that she staved off regret while she toured his vast estate. His behavior, a penchant for pride and arrogance, had certainly not changed since her rebuke. She would console herself with that thought while she tiptoed through his grounds, with its proprietor none the wiser. Honestly, she would not be satisfied until they were off the estate, far enough away that the specter of Mr. Darcy would cease haunting her.

Miss Bennet approached the bank, standing in between two copses of trees. It was a very fine lake, picturesque, and greatly improved the vista. It probably had many turtles in it. She hated turtles ever since one bit her as a child. Her eyes trod along the bank around the lake then she took in a breath of surprise. There were sheep milling about the opposite bank. A smile formed on her face as she thought of the owner's wrath at sheep having full run of his grounds. She snickered at the image of the sheep flouting the proud owner's regulations.

From around the copse of trees to her left emerged a drenched figure of a man with his shirt untucked, holding a similarly soaked coat. The man's head was bent toward the ground but jerked up at her gasp.

Even though his wet hair was stuck to the sides of his face, she would recognize that profile anywhere. It was one she had thought she would never see her entire life again. And had especially not wanted to see here, on the grounds of his estate.

Mr. Darcy paled, nearly equaling the color of his sodden shirt, as he froze in shock.

"Mr. Darcy!" she cried, scarcely able to catch her breath.

"Miss Bennet. I…"

Elizabeth grasped her skirts. "I did not anticipate seeing you…sir. We understood all the family was away, or we should never have presumed…."

"Er, I returned a day early." He hoisted the soaked clothing in front of him, then, with a glance, hurriedly lowered it again, attempting to hide it behind his leg. "I beg your pardon. Your parents are in good health?"

"Er, yes. They are very well. I thank you, sir."

"I'm glad to hear it. How long have you been in this part of the country?"

"But two days, sir."

"And where are you lodging?"

"At the inn at Lambton."

"Oh, yes, of course. Mm…Well, I am…I have just arrived myself. Mm…and your parents are in good health? An…and all your sisters?"

Elizabeth's lips twitched. "Yes. They are all in optimum health, sir."

Mr. Darcy shifted his weight, looking around uneasily. Elizabeth could not stop gawking at his chest as his shirt was sheer. She looked down at the ground, but that caused her gaze to traverse down his chest. She moved her eyes quicker, but then his wet and tight breeches ensnared her focus. Her mouth dropped open as she whirled her head to look at the lake, hoping he could not see her blush.

She backed away to put more distance between them. Meeting the man whose proposal she had rejected was the worst possible situation. Elizabeth's face felt blazing hot. She yearned to run straight for the Gardiners' carriage, close the doors and hide like a young girl playing hide and go seek. Elizabeth peered at his face, then rapidly away.

"What the devil—no!"

A quick look at Mr. Darcy was all she had before she was struck from behind with such force that she lost her balance and fell into the lake.

Gasping, she raised her head and then shoved her ruined hair out of her face while she pulled her legs underneath her. She stood on the soft mud, feeling herself sinking. Teetering, she waved her arms to steady herself.

"Miss Bennet! Remain there. Do not move! Or you will sink further into the mud."

She sniffed and wiped her face, thankful that her back was facing him. Elizabeth glanced down at her gown, mortified. It was ruined and muddy, with bits of leaves and other undergrowth attached.

"Get out of here, you brute!"

At his yell, Elizabeth failed to obey Mr. Darcy's instructions. She twisted her upper body, but her boot was stuck in the mud. While she flailed her arms about like a nincompoop, she glimpsed a large sheep near the bank. Most probably the one that had propelled her into the water. Mr. Darcy was striving to push it away, yelling, but the obstinate sheep refused to move and stood at the edge of the lake, gawping at her.

Cautiously she pulled one boot up at a time and faced the bank. There was a distance of several feet between her and dry ground. She did not know how to walk that distance through the lake up to her waist with the sticky mud, but her fear was relieved when Mr. Darcy advanced to the bank carrying a long branch.

"Miss Bennet, grasp this, and I will draw you out. It is quite difficult to get out of the lake on your own."

Mr. Darcy strode several steps into the water so her outstretched hands could reach the branch. Elizabeth realized this must have been how he had become drenched as well. What were all the sheep doing on his grounds? She suppressed a giggle at their shared predicament and focused on keeping balanced on her feet. She did wish to plunge into the lake again. One time was enough.

She clutched tightly to the coarse bark, hoping the slender end did not split off. Struggling to wrest one leg out of the mud, she had sunk further into the bottom of the lake. She relied on Mr. Darcy's strength to uphold her weight should she fall. Finally, the mud let go, and she wobbled horribly, crying out until she swung her leg forward and sank deep into the muck.

They repeated this perverse dance step by step as Mr. Darcy struggled to remain on sturdy footing while Elizabeth battled the mud.

And that was how her aunt and uncle found them.

CHAPTER 3

*C*ries of alarm jolted Mr. Darcy as he abruptly spun towards the bank. Except the lower half of his body stayed put, so firmly entrenched was the mud's hold on his boots. Arms waving, he dropped the branch before falling backward with a massive splash, soaking Elizabeth in muddy lake water. Again.

Elizabeth yelped, "Beware the sheep! That is how I ended up in the lake."

Mr. Darcy shot out of the lake and stood dripping water and aquatic plant life. Battling himself from uttering any oaths he desperately wanted to say, he wiped his muddy hands on his soiled breeches. Once more, he swept sodden hair out of his eyes, removing leaves from a water plant covering his right cheek. Repulsed, he tossed it back down into the lake.

He glanced at Elizabeth, who was again bright red. Sighing heavily, he turned towards the well-dressed, respectable-looking couple standing at the bank of the lake, both stunned. Most likely, they had been touring Pemberley and did not expect to find the owner standing in the lake. But, perhaps they did not recognize him.

"The Master himself, I presume," said the unfamiliar man.

"And just as handsome as his portrait. Though, perhaps, a little less formally attired," said the woman.

Mr. Darcy closed his eyes and groaned under his breath. Heat flooded his cheeks, an occurrence that he had not experienced since he was at Cambridge. He had entered his room to find it unexpectedly occupied by his roommate, Wickham, and a less-than-reputable woman.

At the muffle behind him, he whirled. Elizabeth was still trapped in the lake up to her waist, but now her hands covered her face. He quickly glanced at her nearly transparent gown and lowered his head before rubbing his hands down his face. He should have shouted for help or hurled his jacket for her to cover herself like a gentleman. Her past accusation *"...if you had behaved in a more gentlemanlike manner..."* echoed in his mind.

Mr. Darcy dropped his hands with a sigh. His coat was on the bank where he had dropped it. The couple in front of him began to chuckle, and Mr. Darcy suddenly understood they knew Miss Bennet. Stuck in the lake, improperly attired, was not how he had hoped to ever be introduced to her respectable friends.

He cleared his throat while turning towards the woman who would no doubt disdain to never speak to him again. "Would you do me the honor of introducing me to your friends?"

Elizabeth started, quickly lowering her hands. "Certainly. Mr. and Mrs. Edward Gardiner, Mr. Darcy." Her uncle removed his hat. "They are my aunt and uncle."

Mr. Darcy bowed. "Delighted to make your acquaintance, Madam."

Mrs. Gardiner curtsied while Mr. Gardiner bowed. "Delighted, sir."

The situation's absurdity was almost too much for Mr. Darcy to bear. He covered his mouth with his fist while studying the rippling water surrounding his knees.

Giggling wafted on the air from behind him.

Mr. Darcy began to offer an explanation. "Please pardon my attire. One of my tenants is having some problems with his flock today. Beware the renegade sheep wandering about. They will not hesitate to push you into the lake with us." The Gardiners exchanged glances as muffled laughter from the lake reached him once more. He cleared his throat. "If you would be so kind, could you go to the house and let Mrs. Reynolds, or anyone, know that we need assistance?"

"Yes." Mr. Gardiner patted his wife's arm, then turned to dash up the slight incline that led to the steps of the terrace.

Mr. Darcy sighed at the shrewd gaze of Mrs. Gardiner glancing between him and Elizabeth. He kept his eyes averted and on the grass of the bank instead of picking up the long branch and continuing to try to pull Elizabeth out of the lake. He was certain Mrs. Gardiner would not want his eyes on her niece's figure, so he stood knee-deep in his lake like a roly-poly waiting for help to arrive.

The time passed excruciatingly slowly, but it did pass, and soon the thuds of footmen running across the lawn reached them. "Sir, we brought a lead line from the stables. We thought it the best tool to pull you out."

"Good thinking. But Miss Bennet will be helped first." Mr. Darcy reached out. "Throw it here!"

He caught the rope, wrapped it around his left arm, and slowly trudged in the mud deeper into the lake towards Elizabeth. She peered up through her wet hair, arms clutched across her chest. He turned his head and yelled at the footmen on the bank. "Turn around and show your backs to Miss Bennet! Pull on the rope when I give the order."

Facing her again, he trudged through the muck until he was close enough to wrap the rope around her. He fought the urge to touch her, to slide his fingers over her hips, the side of her waist. Leaning close to tie a sturdy knot, he breathed deeply and caught her scent that had tantalized him so in Hertfordshire.

And again at Rosings. He clenched his fingers hard on the coarse rope as he made the final tie-off.

He had thought the next time he would see her, if he ever did, it would be a cheerful smile and approval of his gentlemanly behavior. Not covered in lake scum and drenched. Blast those sheep. Being humiliated and thrown in his lake would no doubt further secure her feelings against him.

Avoiding her gaze, he turned his head. "Pull now! Slowly."

He held out his arm. "Hold on to me. The mud does not give up its prizes easily."

She flashed him a quick smile before placing her dainty hand on his muddy forearm. "You think I am a prize, Mr. Darcy?"

He sputtered and was saved from having to answer by the sudden lurch of the rope as the footmen began to pull. Elizabeth's grip on his arm tightened as she was yanked forwards, throwing her off balance. She recovered quickly, and with the added momentum of the footmen on the bank, it was easier for her to pull her boots out of the mud with each step. Mr. Darcy stayed by her side, lending his arm for her to hold on to as she steadily approached the bank and safety.

Once they were both on solid ground, Mr. Darcy quickly untied the rope around Elizabeth's waist. It would have been a task for one of the servants. But he did not want anyone else to stand that close to her, brush their fingers against her body, or feel her heat.

He cleared his throat and then raised his head while stepping back, but one look at her bedraggled state stopped him in his tracks. Her once pristine dress was now stained with mud and clinging to her body in a most unbecoming way. Her hair was plastered to her head, with leaves and grass tangled amongst the tresses. She looked like a drowned rat. Mr. Darcy's heart sank as he realized she could not have a good opinion of him after this.

"Quickly, wrap the blanket around her," said Mrs. Gardiner. She addressed the housekeeper who had joined the crowd of servants. "Please have our carriage pulled out front." She then turned towards Elizabeth after a shallow curtsy as her husband bowed.

"Thank you for rescuing our niece from the lake. I do not want to imagine what could have befallen her if you had not been here to save her." Mr. Gardiner glanced away, seeming to resolve himself, then faced him directly again. "We have matters to discuss. I will call upon you after my niece has been cared for and situated." Another bow and Mr. Gardiner turned to follow his wife and niece already several feet ahead of him up the hill.

Mr. Darcy stilled, staring at the backs of Elizabeth Bennet and her relatives. Everything felt tilted off its axis as if he had been knocked off his feet by a sheep again. He battled the urge to pursue them, worried he would never see Elizabeth again.

"You cannot—"

The Gardiners paused and looked back, shock plain on their faces. But the one face he wanted to see was still facing away from him.

"Miss Bennet will catch a chill. Lambton is too far a distance after recently falling in a lake. I will have the physician summoned to ensure she is well after she has warmed up and changed." Mr. Darcy finished speaking in his Master of Pemberley voice and was confused when Mr. Gardiner did not flinch.

Instead, Elizabeth's uncle looked to his wife, who raised her eyebrow, and Mr. Gardiner cleared his throat.

Suddenly, Mr. Darcy realized his faux pas. "If you agree, that is, sir."

At this, Elizabeth turned around and rewarded Mr. Darcy with a small smile and nod.

He glanced at Mrs. Reynolds, who nodded in return.

"Return to the house and prepare a hot bath for Miss Bennet in the yellow room. Have Sally find a gown for her."

"Oh, we could not impose," stated Mr. Gardiner. "Lambton is but—"

"Nonsense, I insist. It is my fault. My sheep pushed her into the lake. It would be remiss of me to not call a doctor and keep her from getting ill. You must stay."

The Gardiners shared a glance, but he was most concerned as to Elizabeth's thoughts on the matter. But her head was bowed, her shoulders hunched as if she was thoroughly embarrassed. He did not know what to say to assuage her mind. She had done nothing to warrant that feeling. He was the one that was mortified.

"Thank you," said Mr. Gardiner with a bow of his head. "For your hospitality. We will gladly take you up on your offer."

Mr. Darcy could not miss Elizabeth's swift turn of her head towards her uncle. Or her widened eyes. But she uttered not a word, faced towards Pemberley again. She trudged awkwardly even quicker uphill, with her boots slipping on the wet grass and a large blanket swaddling her body.

He hastened up the hill, determined to speed through a cold bath and dress swiftly so Elizabeth could see him as a respectable gentleman. It might not have any bearing. The day's events had likely turned her from ever considering him again. Still, he would not pass up this opportunity.

Mr. Darcy ran across the foyer, up the curved staircase, and down the hall to his bed-chamber. He did not know how Mrs. Reynolds would find a gown to fit Elizabeth as his sister was taller and had less of a womanly figure.

His valet stepped into the room. "Your bath should be ready shortly, sir."

Mr. Darcy ripped off his ruined shirt. "Have Miss Bennet's bath prepared before mine," he commanded. "And have the modiste summoned with a gown to be altered for Miss Bennet."

"The housekeeper has already dispatched Miss Bennet's clothing from the inn in Lambton."

Mr. Darcy shook his head and then continued undressing. Of course, she would desire her own clothing. Why was he dissatisfied that he could not provide for her? He barely refrained from swearing at the misstep he had nearly made. Purchasing her clothing would have been a dreadful insult. It would have implied she was his mistress.

Truthfully, he yearned for her as his wife.

But she had resolutely rejected his proposal in Hunsford and had been knocked into the lake by one of his sheep. Indeed, matters could not become worse.

CHAPTER 4

*E*lizabeth kept her head down and tugged the blanket as high on her head as she could to hide her face. It had not felt so humiliating when it had just been her and Mr. Darcy, both drenched and muddy from being pushed into the lake by a sheep. But when her aunt and uncle had arrived, as well as servants…all she wanted to do was flee at once.

But Mr. Darcy, who continued to bewilder her, was ever the kind gentleman. A far cry from his haughty behavior from before. Instead of displaying his previous conceited conduct and dismissing her immediately, he insisted she stay to bathe and change clothing. Elizabeth would have to confront him again, thank him when she would rather hide in their carriage.

"Your cheeks are flaming. I fear you may be ill already," stated the housekeeper, who gestured to a servant. "Rebecca, remove her boots. Quickly, now!"

The maid at Longbourn had never assisted them with their footwear. It was mortifying to have one of Mr. Darcy's servants see the worn state of her walking boots and the slightly frayed hem in the back that showed the age of her dress. But perhaps the mud from the lake camouflaged it completely?

Elizabeth clamped her lips together to suppress the smile struggling to form. No one would think she should be smiling at her situation and would likely ponder if she was a candidate for Bedlam.

The maid shrieked and recoiled while a little fish in lake water glided out of Elizabeth's upturned boot. Elizabeth closed her eyes, unsure how she would survive the embarrassing situations still yet to come. And then water splashed her foot as the maid picked up her foot and scrubbed it, so she would not sully the floor inside the grand estate. Indeed, nothing could be worse than this.

Mrs. Reynolds guided her to the second floor, which had not been included in the earlier tour. Elizabeth glanced down the hall, the other wing of the house, but it looked the same as the wing she was being directed down. This yellow guest room was so opulently appointed she could not imagine what the family's bedrooms looked like. Indeed, she was beginning to understand why Miss Bingley longed to form an attraction with Mr. Darcy. But the trappings of wealth did not interest her, only love. At least, that's what she continued to tell herself as she stood on a delicate rug while a large copper tub was filled with hot water. At Longbourn, they had one servant and a cramped, darkened tub.

Elizabeth stayed hidden in the blanket until the bathing screen was placed in front of the tub. Rapidly she divested herself of her sodden wet underthings, which the maid did not even let touch the silky smooth rug before she quit the room. Then she slowly submerged into the hot bath and covered her face to muffle the sounds of her laughter.

She did not laugh in the bathing tub, as a rule. But it was either that or weep. And she would not cry, not over something so ludicrous as running into Mr.

Darcy at his estate when he was supposed to have been away! And then having one of his sheep push her into the lake. It was the most absurd farce. She snorted and muffled her mouth. Ripples sprawled out from her body as she labored to contain her laughter.

But then the laughter abated as the sadness surfaced. Mr. Darcy had changed his behavior, but he could not still have feelings for her. Not now, not after he had discovered her exploring his estate. How embarrassing. Elizabeth covered her face again. But she did not stay sad for long. Indeed it was not even a minute before she was back to her usual self. Albeit, more concerned with leaving the premises without delay.

She blotted her eyes, though her hands were wet from the bath water, and indeed her eyes were now damper than before, but it had made her feel better. Elizabeth had resilience, but even the most stoic would admit how terribly this visit to tour Pemberley had gone. Jane would never believe it. She would write her sister immediately upon arrival back at the inn.

Elizabeth groaned at the thought of journeying to Lambton, with her aunt and uncle sending her pitying looks. She could not endure it. But she would rather suffer their pitied looks than staying in Mr. Darcy's well-appointed guest room. One of his guest rooms was in a wing of his house dedicated to visitors. She must leave at once before he had dressed and was waiting for their party.

Swiftly, she bathed, dunking her head in the water and dragging her fingers through her hair to remove any improper grass and other lake debris. Elizabeth stood, grabbed a towel, and realized she could not leave the room with her hair undone. But that would not stop her from leaving Mr. Darcy's home. She rubbed her hair until she could not get more water out of it. Then she dried herself off and extended her arm for her dress on the bed, but it was not her dress.

A maid's uniform was laid out on the bed. She gaped as her cheeks grew warm. This was the most embarrassing experience of her life. The housekeeper must have thought she was nobody. Perhaps she thought Elizabeth was a poor relation on tour with relatives. It did not signify spending any more thoughts on the subject. She just needed clothing to depart the room and reach Gardiners' carriage before Mr. Darcy dressed. How much time had she spent in the tub?

Elizabeth tossed on the dress but could not fasten all the buttons on the back. It would have to do. Braiding her hair, she surveyed the room and saw the wet blanket she used on her walk to the house still on the floor. Frowning, she picked it up and wrapped it about her shoulders. It would mask the unfastened part of her back and would have to do.

She stepped across the soft, plush rug to the door and peeked out. So strong was her urgent need to depart that on any other occasion, she would have never considered scurrying through Pemberley with her bare feet. Her boots must still be on the terrace by the front door. Or moved to the service entrance.

On that thought, she braced her nerves and then crept out into the hallway. She thanked her blessings that she encountered no one. Slowing her stride, she stepped as silently as she could down the curved staircase in the foyer. The dress was sliding off her shoulder. All she needed to do was reach the front door. Then she would be in the carriage, and they could quit this uncomfortable nightmare.

She stepped quickly across the foyer, purposely not looking at the footmen stationed by the front door.

"Lizzy! Lizzy, is that you?"

Elizabeth stopped, her bare feet squealing against the white marble floor, and spun toward the direction of the call. Mrs. Gardiner was in front of an open doorway, a horrified expression upon her face.

"Lizzy, what are you doing?"

She had never seen her aunt so shocked before and nearly speechless.

"Let us go to the carriage and depart immediately. Please."

Her uncle joined her aunt in the foyer. His eyes had never been so wide.

"Please, uncle, let us rush back to the inn. Oh, I wish we had never come."

Mr. and Mrs. Gardiner exchanged a lingering look. It was clear her aunt had reservations, but she followed her husband toward the entrance and motioned for Elizabeth to join them. Once outside, she let out a relieved breath, stepped into her soggy boots without tying the laces, and carefully descended the steps to their carriage on the drive. A waiting footman opened the door and assisted her, raising an eyebrow at her attire.

She snuggled deeper into the blanket, then turned her head away from the house, wishing she could make herself invisible. Elizabeth couldn't bear any more humiliation today. Or this trip. Or probably the year.

"All right, Smith," declared Mr. Gardiner to their driver. "We should be off to the inn."

Elizabeth allowed herself to relax; everything would be fine. They would depart as soon as her uncle stepped into the carriage after helping her aunt up. And Mr. Darcy wouldn't know a thing.

The carriage jolted, then her aunt settled beside her on the bench without haste. "Lizzy," she whispered, "you are undressed! You could have been seen by Mr. Darcy!"

"That's why I wanted us to leave immediately, so he would not see me!"

Her aunt gave her a probing glance, frowning. "Was he unhappy? What did he say?

Elizabeth compressed her lips. "Nothing of importance. He asked about my parents…."

A faint noise from behind startled her. The sound of pounding footsteps quickly descending the stairs of

Pemberley alarmed her. She attempted to steady her breathing while she pulled the blanket over her head.

"Miss Bennet!"

CHAPTER 5

*M*r. Darcy had completed his bath in record time. His valet dressed him quickly but not fast enough. Mr. Darcy dashed out of his bedroom, fastening one of his cufflinks as his long strides devoured the distance to the main staircase.

"Miss Bennet, where is she? The blue sitting room?"

The startled maid dropped into a curtsy. "No, sir. Er, she departed."

He stopped still and felt as if time slowed to a trickle. "Departed?"

Time snapped back while he sprinted down the curved staircase across the expansive foyer. He stormed out the front door that the footmen held open for him. And there was her carriage, with her uncle just climbing in. Elizabeth's head was turned away. Why was she swaddled in that sodden, dirty blanket again? Did she not bathe?

His boots pounding on the stone steps, he did not take these steps quite as swiftly as he had the staircase inside. It would not impress Elizabeth if he stumbled and tumbled down the entire flight. But he could not let her leave without speaking to her.

"Miss Bennet!"

Mr. and Mrs. Gardiner's heads swiveled towards him as he hastened down the stone steps. Since his last glance at her a few seconds ago, Elizabeth had pulled the blanket over her head. He frowned, unsure as to why she thought she needed to hide. She had done nothing to disgrace herself.

"Please allow me to apologize for not receiving you properly just now. You are not leaving?"

Elizabeth's aunt shared a look with her husband, who answered for them. "We were, sir. I think we must."

"I hope you are not displeased with Pemberley." He had directed his question to the blanket-covered woman who refused to turn towards him.

After a peek at her niece, Mrs. Gardiner whispered. "Lizzy!"

Finally, the woman that had graced his dreams faced him. She still looked pale. "No, not at all."

"Then you approve of it?

She smiled. Mr. Darcy's chest lightened. "Very much. But I think few would not approve."

"But your good opinion is rarely bestowed and, therefore, more worth the earning."

"Thank you." She looked at her aunt and uncle, her eyes pleading.

"You are staying in Lambton, I hear."

Elizabeth's aunt responded. "Yes, sir. I grew up there as a girl."

With no more response forthcoming and Elizabeth not looking at him again, Mr. Darcy clenched his hands behind his back. "I…I had hoped you would stay for supper. You are not leaving because my staff did not attend to your needs?"

Finally, she turned her head towards him again. Her brown eyes looked like a fine chestnut horse in the sun's light. "I believe we must."

"Please allow me to make amends for my ornery sheep. I would like to invite you to dine here with a party of my friends arriving tomorrow. One party member is quite eager to meet you, Miss Bennet. I would be honored if you and your aunt and uncle would be my guests for supper. Would tomorrow evening be convenient?"

She glanced down with a faint blush, then looked up at him directly. "We shall be delighted."

Hearing a male clear his throat, Mr. Darcy dragged his gaze to her uncle. "I would like to meet with you regarding a matter of business after seeing the ladies settled at the inn."

Mr. Darcy's lips tightened, but he had been expecting it. It was not an unwelcome meeting, not for him at least. But, it was embarrassing that he would wed Elizabeth due to being compromised by his infuriating sheep. He would not know if she genuinely cared for him.

He nodded to Mr. Gardiner, then banged twice on the carriage door, a signal every driver knew. Mr.

Darcy stood there tracking the carriage until it rolled around the bend of the lake and out of sight.

Mr. Darcy sighed and rubbed his face. Then he slowly turned and climbed up the steps like a man going to his execution. He entered his office and closed the door behind him. He was not given to drink, but this occasion warranted it if any did. He poured a finger of Scottish whiskey and downed it. Standing, staring at nothing, he lost track of time. Then he poured himself another finger of whiskey and sat in his chair.

He had hoped to dazzle Elizabeth the next time he saw her, and now her uncle would demand he marry his niece because they had been compromised. Mr. Darcy could not deny that Elizabeth's gown was scandalously sheer. His anger renewed as he recalled several of his servants ogling her before his command to avert their eyes.

THE GARDINER'S carriage stopped at the Lambton Inn with Elizabeth still huddled under the blanket. Her uncle instructed their driver to pull up at the servant's entrance to keep her state of dishabille hidden. Nothing untoward had occurred between her and Mr. Darcy. Still, when an eligible young woman arrived looking as she did, the inn's proprietor would be within his rights to have her ejected. This was not that type of establishment.

She clasped the blanket tightly, leaping out of the carriage and darting into the inn. It was not hard to find the servant's staircase to the upper floor where her room was, as it was directly to the left once Elizabeth got her bearings. Her hands shook as she rushed to her room and slammed the door shut. If anyone had seen her and recognized her, she would have been ruined instead of just compromised.

But her compromise could be kept quiet. Only her family and Mr. Darcy needed to know. If word got out that Elizabeth Bennet had been seen in a state of undress, her hair disheveled, that was something she did not want to contemplate. That gossip could have far-reaching effects, such as ruining her sisters' chances of ever finding eligible suitors.

She ripped off the blanket and tossed it on the floor. It should be burned. Or would Mr. Darcy expect it returned? Turning, Elizabeth massaged her face and plopped on the edge of her bed. How lucky were they that only Mr. Darcy had arrived a day early? A large party would be coming the next day! If Miss Bingley had seen her…her reputation would have been ruined completely. She could envision the sneer on that woman's face, having seen it many times in Hertfordshire.

After a sharp tap at the door, she raised her head to see her aunt enter and blanch. "Lizzy, what are you wearing?"

Elizabeth closed her eyes. She had forgotten what she was wearing. Her plan had been to change into one of her other gowns before her relatives saw her. But it was too late now.

"Did they really dress you in a maid's uniform? I am surprised a servant, especially one at Pemberley, would have attired you in such a manner. And allowed you to leave the room!"

Opening her eyes for a peek, they quickly widened when she saw how perturbed her aunt was. "The gown was lying on the bed when I finished my bath. No maid was present; they must have intended to return, but I wanted to depart immediately."

Mrs. Gardiner had never looked so stern. "No maid to help you! I waited in the sitting room, thinking you had several servants assisting you. I had expected better from a gentleman's household. Especially one such as Pemberley."

She looked weary from the thought of such ill-treatment to her niece and settled in the chair facing the bed. "I had commanded the modiste in Lambton to be sent for. I specifically remember mentioning it to the housekeeper." The older woman frowned, her ire replaced by worry. "This is a scandal, Lizzy. On top of the one you were already part of. A gentleman's daughter dressed as a servant; it is unheard of. I am glad your uncle will speak to Mr. Darcy yet today."

Elizabeth did not want an awkward situation made worse by her uncle dressing down Mr. Darcy. Not when he would already be displeased that he would be forced to marry her. Oh, how she wished they had never visited Pemberley.

She stood and approached her aunt, still standing by the door. "I cannot conceive that the housekeeper who had seemed so kind would do such a thing. Most likely, it was something to wear until the modiste arrived."

Mrs. Gardiner pursed her lips. "It is still not proper. You could have worn a robe and stayed in the room. To have you don a servant's dress, then send you out with your hair braided so unkempt… this is worse than any behavior I would have expected from that man based on your stories of his conduct in Hertfordshire."

"Aunt, do not blame him. I braided my hair without waiting for a maid. I wanted to quit Pemberley before Mr. Darcy saw me again. And truly this could not be Mr. Darcy's doing. He was a gentleman today, he would have never ordered or permitted this. But no one saw me and my reputation is still intact."

Her aunt did not look placated but thankfully dropped the subject. "I will speak with your uncle before he departs for Pemberley."

CHAPTER 6

M r. Darcy stared at the amber liquid in his crystal glass. He had been in high spirits arriving home that morning, and then it had all descended into a debacle of the worst kind. At the thought of what Elizabeth must think of him now, considering she had covered her head and nearly refused to look at him, he downed the contents of his glass.

Tapping at the door announced Mrs. Reynold's entrance. "You called for me, sir?"

He gauged his housekeeper. "Did something happen to Miss Bennet?"

Mrs. Reynolds was uncharacteristically flustered. "She… she chose to leave."

"Do you know why she was wrapped up in the dirty blanket given to her at the lake?"

The woman wrung her hands. "I do not, sir. Her clothes had not even arrived yet from Lambton. I have ordered—"

Knocking interrupted the interrogation, much to Mr. Darcy's irritation. "Enter!"

A maid, young with thick black hair piled on the back of her head, entered and, after a glance at him, lowered her head.

Mrs. Reynolds pinched her lips when the maid entered. "What did you do to Miss Bennet? Explain yourself!"

He had never seen the housekeeper in such a mood before.

The maid flinched. "I did what you told me to. I fetched Abigail's dress. I laid it on the bed in the guest room where Miss Bennet was taking her bath."

Mr. Darcy frowned. He did not know any member of his staff with that name. "Abigail's dress?"

"Yes, sir." She clenched her hands so tightly that her knuckles were white. "Abigail, the Cook. Mrs. Reynolds told me—"

"I did no such thing! I would have never—"

"Stop, please. Mrs. Reynolds, if I am to sort out this matter, I need to hear an accounting from the maid. Please, continue." Mr. Darcy perched on the edge of his chair, eager to ascertain why Miss Bennet had declined to stay at Pemberley until her trunk was delivered from Lambton.

The maid burst into tears. Her face quickly transformed from pale white to red and blotchy. It was evident she would not continue her story unless prompted. "Maid—what is your name? I cannot address you as a maid."

The young maid tried to get herself under control, but not fast enough for Mrs. Reynolds. "She is Sally. I promoted her to upstairs maid several weeks ago, a mistake, to be sure."

Hard crying recommenced at that pronouncement.

Mr. Darcy sighed. "Mrs. Reynolds, could you please wait in the hall? I fear I will not get the full accounting with you present."

The housekeeper twitched her skirts, then, with a slight nod, she swept out of the study, closing the door behind her.

"Now, Sally, please calm yourself."

She sobbed harder.

Mr. Darcy rubbed a hand down his face. He should have remembered the other times he had tried to assuage a female by telling her to calm down. It never ever had worked and indeed had only made matters worse.

"Sally, have a seat and pour yourself a cup of tea. I would like to hear what Mrs. Reynolds' orders were for you. I know you completed the task exactly how you were requested, which is why I am eager to hear the instructions you were given."

That did the trick. Sally wiped her eyes, still breathing heavily from her strenuous crying. After composing herself and several sips of tea, she glanced up at Mr. Darcy before her gaze darted down to the cup in her hands. "It was like I said, sir. Mrs. Reynolds commanded me to get Abigail's gown and take it to Miss Bennet."

He scowled, knowing his housekeeper could not have uttered those instructions. Yet this young girl was adamant it had. She was too distraught and shocked at Mrs. Reynold's denial to be lying. "Could you repeat exactly what Mrs. Reynolds said? Word for word."

"Abigail, get a dress in Miss Bennet's size and bring it to her."

Mr. Darcy groaned and slumped back in his chair. This explained why Elizabeth had fled, hiding under a blanket, if he was correct.

"Please, ask Mrs. Reynolds to enter."

After the housekeeper returned, full of starch, Mr. Darcy rubbed his face. He willed himself not to laugh at the sheer absurdity of one day.

"I believe I have solved the problem," Mr. Darcy declared. He looked at Mrs. Reynolds' stern face before fixing his gaze on the still blotchy young maid, Sally. "You have moved from Wales recently?"

She nodded. "Yes, sir."

"Did you know that Abigail is a common word in England to mean lady's maid?" Confusion overwhelmed Sally's face, far better than the fear and shame that had replaced it. "So when Mrs. Reynolds said Abigail, she meant you, not the Cook, Abigail. Cook is Cook."

Sally burst into tears again.

Mrs. Reynolds was gobsmacked. "I never—that was certainly not what I meant, Mr. Darcy! I would—" she turned to the maid in horror. "Sally, what dress did you give her?"

Sally sobbed harder.

Mr. Darcy leaned an elbow on the desk and rested his head in his hand.

"Why," stated Mrs. Reynolds in a voice much louder than usual, "did you not stop to think! You know I would never order you to bring a servant's uniform for any guest to wear!"

"I could not question your orders, Mrs. Reynolds!"

Knocking at the door to his study joined the pounding in his head. He sat up straight in his wing-back chair. "Enter!"

A footman, holding a bag, stepped in. He could not keep his eyes off the hysterically crying maid.

"Yes, Mr. Entwhistle?"

"I, er, have the clothing for Miss Bennet, sir. From the Lambton Inn."

Mr. Darcy closed his eyes, wishing this was a farcical nightmare and he would awaken. He opened his eyes to find the same scene, except the footman was now gaping at him. "Thank you. However, Miss Bennet departed without waiting for her clothing. Please, return it directly."

The footman opened his mouth and quickly closed it. After another glance at the weeping maid, he quit the room, closing the door behind him.

The glass of whiskey beckoning called to him, but Mr. Darcy pushed it aside. He was not given to drink; even though today was quite trying, he would not succumb to that vice.

A loud sniffle caught his attention. "Will… will I be dismissed?"

Mr. Darcy answered quickly before the housekeeper could. "No, you will not be dismissed. It was an… understandable mistake."

"Thank you so much, Mr. Dar—"

Knocking at the door interrupted the maid. Mr. Darcy withheld himself from groaning at the slightest of margins. "Enter."

"There is a Mr. Gardiner here for you, sir," announced a footman.

Mr. Darcy rubbed his face. This was not at all in any manner how he had expected this day to go. It was a never-ending nightmare.

"Wait a few minutes, then send him in," he ordered the footman. "Sally, you are dismissed. Mrs. Reynolds, stay. I would not think Mr. Gardiner would believe... this... Sally?"

The maid was swaying and appeared as if she had seen a ghost. Then she burst into tears. Again. "You said you were not going to dismiss me. My Mam will be—"

Mr. Darcy jumped up from his chair, ready to catch the deathly pale young maid swaying where she stood. "No, you misunderstood me. You are not dismissed as in—sacked. You are still employed here as an upstairs maid. I am just dismissing you from my presence. From this room."

He reached the young maid and touched her arms to assure her he was genuine.

And that was how Mr. Gardiner found them. "Upon my word!"

Mr. Darcy stepped back from the maid, who had thankfully stopped crying. After a quick explanation regarding Sally's tears, which led to an explanation of how a maid's uniform was mistakenly given to Miss Bennet, Mr. Gardiner no longer looked ready to pummel Mr. Darcy with his walking stick.

"That is quite the tale." Mr. Gardiner glanced at the maid, who had started sniffling again.

"I assure you, Mr. Gardiner, it was never my intention to insult your niece in this manner—indeed— Sally, please stop crying. You are not dismissed. Go to the kitchens for luncheon." He turned to Mr. Gardiner. "Unless you have had any more questions regarding Miss Bennet's care while she was under my roof?"

Mr. Gardiner cleared his throat. "Indeed, I do. Your maid from Wales, not understanding that Abigail meant lady's maid, is understandable. But it does not signify why no maid was present to braid my niece's hair nor button up her dress."

Mr. Darcy's gaze darted to Sally, who blanched.

"Sally, do you have an explanation for this?"

The young maid, now reddening, wrung her hands as she stared down at the rug under her boots and mumbled a response.

Mrs. Reynolds placed her hand on the girl's shoulder. "Speak up; we cannot hear you."

The girl sniffled and answered while her head was still lowered. "I thought she would be in the bath longer, sir. I needed…" her voice grew faint, barely able to hear, but the words were unmistakable. "Needed to use the lavatory."

Mr. Darcy closed his eyes, wishing he could vanish. He sighed, then opened his eyes and hoped he had, if not a pleasant, then not a terrifying visage. The young maid had been tormented enough. "Thank you, Sally. Please, go to the kitchen and have your luncheon now."

Sally curtsied and dashed out of the room as if her skirts were ablaze.

Mr. Darcy massaged his forehead. He could not envisage another episode that could have put him in a worse light than the series of incidents that had transpired that day. "Mrs. Reynolds, could you order tea? Mr. Gardiner, please take a seat."

Mrs. Reynolds quit the room, and Mr. Gardiner slumped heavily in the wingback chair in front of Mr. Darcy's desk. The only sounds in the room were the fire crackling and the grandfather clock ticking. After several minutes, Mrs. Reynolds ushered a footman into the study with the tea tray and sandwiches. Mr. Darcy had it stationed on the table next to Mr. Gardiner. He could not eat. The events of the day and the loss of Elizabeth's goodwill were weighing heavily on his mind.

Mr. Darcy reclined in his chair as Mr. Gardiner sipped his tea and consumed a cucumber sandwich. He studied the older man who had been genial until his niece had been propelled into Mr. Darcy's lake. He would not be astonished if Mr. Gardner did not want his niece attached to a man whose estate was in such disarray.

"Well," said Mr. Gardner while wiping crumbs off his hands with a serviette, "that clarifies quite a bit. The poor maid must have been beside herself, supposing she would be discharged. And I am impressed that you showed such concern for a servant."

Mr. Darcy wanted to explain that his family always held a good reputation with their staff but held back. He realized Mr. Gardiner did not intend any insult. "Yes, she was nearly inconsolable."

Mr. Darcy cleared his throat, feeling abashed. But it was not every day that you encountered a young lady's guardian to work out a marriage contract after one of your sheep compromised you and the young lady. He allowed his words to be of what most concerned him.

"How is Miss Bennet? She has not caught a chill?"

Mr. Gardiner picked up another cucumber sandwich. "Oh, no. My niece has an indomitable constitution. Once she changed clothes, she was back to her usual spirits." He scarfed it in two bites, gulped his tea, then lowered the teacup to the table and leveled a direct gaze upon the younger man. "My wife and I found you and my niece in the lake together. Her clothing was... well, I know you are a reputable gentleman. I trust you will you do the honorable thing?"

Mr. Darcy esteemed a man that did not squander breath and knew their judgment. The sooner he could finish this uncomfortable conversation, the better. "Yes. There is a solicitor in Lambton that will be arriving shortly to draw up the marriage contract. Let us discuss the particulars. I would like the solicitor to conclude our business quickly."

Relief seemed to settle on Mr. Gardiner, who nodded with a smile. His usual jovial nature once again asserted itself. Amicably, he and the wealthiest man in Derbyshire discussed what properties, valuables, and allowance would be settled upon his niece.

CHAPTER 7

*E*lizabeth was quiet during the short journey back to Pemberley, which seemed to fly by, unlike yesterday's tour. The jolt of the footman opening the door and lowering the steps removed her from her reverie.

Then Mr. Darcy stretched into the carriage for her hand, and she paused to stand up from the bench. She had expected more time to compose herself before seeing him again. Especially since her uncle did not tell her or her aunt what transpired during the meeting yesterday.

Elizabeth breathed deeply, plastered on a smile, and accepted his hand. Mr. Darcy helped her down, then placed Elizabeth's hand on his arm and led them up the many steps of Pemberley.

Elizabeth felt her cheeks flush though she had willed herself not to blush. It was prodigiously challenging to pretend she had not been standing before him yesterday, bedraggled, lake scum in her hair, with her gown nearly transparent.

Her gaze did not stray from directly in front of her as they climbed the steps. It was not until they reached the landing that she noticed Mr. Darcy had not spoken either. And now it was too late to break the awkward silence.

Elizabeth removed her hand from his arm after they entered the imposing house. Her slippers tapped on the white marble floor as she walked to stand next to her relatives. The Gardiners' expressions were quite removed from the awe and wonder they had displayed yesterday.

"Please, come into the sitting room," Mr. Darcy requested. "But Miss Bennet, could I request you stay here with me for a moment?"

He looked nervous, a sight she had not seen before, not even at the first assembly in Meryton. Mr. and

Mrs. Gardiner followed Mr. Darcy's request and left their niece in the foyer.

Elizabeth stepped towards the sitting room, just off the foyer to the left, to spy where her relatives were going. It was one of the rooms they saw on the tour yesterday with Mrs. Reynolds. Mr. Darcy reached for her hand, but Elizabeth turned her head away. Yesterday's humiliation dampened her usual cheerful disposition.

Her uncle had remained mum about her new predicament with Mr. Darcy. Still, she did not have to be a learned scholar to suspect the subject of their discussion.

"I must apologize again, Miss Bennet, for the embarrassing situation we found ourselves in yesterday. Never have my sheep behaved so ill."

Her lips turned up at Mr. Darcy apologizing for his livestock. Like her father, she could never stay in too dark a humor when there was an absurdity to laugh at. "Sheep have a mind of their own. Please do not punish them too severely. I am sure he thought my light-colored day dress was another ram encroaching on his territory."

He did not share her smile but instead seemed to steel himself. "Miss Bennet, I... I would be—"

"—I am sure she did not—oh, Mr. Darcy, there you are!"

At the sound of the grating voice they both recognized, Mr. Darcy hastily dropped Elizabeth's hand.

Miss Bingley and her sister smiled and preened as they gracefully glided down the main curved staircase. They hastened directly to Mr. Darcy's side, not even sparing a glance at Elizabeth that she could tell.

Elizabeth stumbled back, her heart beating rapidly. Against all odds, all manner of reason, it had seemed that Mr. Darcy had been about to renew his proposal to her! Even though she had so thoroughly rejected him once before! She took another step back, unable to tear her gaze away from the tableau in front of her. The Bingley sisters were at Pemberley, obviously staying as guests, most likely for at least a month. She was surprised, although she remembered that Mrs. Reynolds had said on their tour that a large party would be arriving the next day.

She was startled by a noise behind her and spun to see what it was. Mrs. Gardiner stood just inside the sitting room, confusion on her face, which grew the longer she took in Elizabeth's demeanor. Mr. Gardiner stepped out into the foyer, his visage changing quickly to a polite smile, but not before she had seen his thoughts clear as day on his face.

Elizabeth had seen that look only once before when Mr. Gardiner had been betrayed by a shipping company that sold products he had ordered to a rival merchant. Products Mr. Gardiner had already paid for from East India. The shipping company had returned Mr. Gardiner's investment, but the damage to his company had not been so easily undone.

Mrs. Gardiner embraced her niece, and Mr. Gardiner followed, standing on Elizabeth's other side.

"Mrs. Hurst, Miss Bingley, you remember Miss Bennet?" Mr. Darcy looked at her again. "And these are her uncle and aunt, Mr. and Mrs. Gardiner from London."

At the mention of the city, Miss Bingley looked at the older couple before turning to her sister. "London? Would they not be the relatives Jane previously mentioned when she had luncheon with us at Netherfield? The ones from Cheapside?"

Miss Bingley sniggered until Mr. Darcy's scolding stare silenced her.

He turned back to Elizabeth and her relatives. "Miss Bennet and the Gardiners are my guests for supper and music afterward. Let us go in the sitting room."

Mr. Darcy advanced towards her, but Miss Bingley would not let go of him and moved with him. But it did not signify, as Elizabeth was in no mind to pay him any attention, even if he looked at her with longing and contrition. Elizabeth stepped away, accompanied by her aunt and uncle, into the sitting room.

Miss Bingley claimed a settee next to a winged armchair, most likely where Mr. Darcy would sit. Mrs. Hurst joined her sister. Mr. Hurst wandered in without speaking to anyone except to ask when supper would be called.

Elizabeth sat on a sofa next to Mr. and Mrs. Gardiner near the Bingley sisters. The two women immediately began an exclusive conversation describing all the latest fashions and diversions they had seen that summer. Which could not have been for Mr. Darcy's benefit, as had he not been with them in London? Finally, Miss Bingley's soliloquy paused, and Elizabeth could ask that very question. Mr. Darcy was not given time to answer before Miss Bingley responded for him.

"My brother Charles, I am sure, will be down soon. He was assisting Miss Darcy with one of the pieces she has been studying on the piano." A sly smile directed at Elizabeth accompanied her address before she turned back to the object of her fixation. "Your sister and my brother have become such good friends while we have been in London. Would you not agree, Mr. Darcy? They are so well-suited to each other; both have such pleasing temperaments."

Elizabeth started when she felt Mrs. Gardiner's hand cover her clenched fists where they rested on her lap. She flattened her hands and pasted a pleasant smile on her face, though she would rather have been anywhere else. Elizabeth knew it would be the height of rudeness to stand up and wander away from this grouping. Still, she could not listen to Miss Bingley discuss her brother's happiness with Mr. Darcy's sister, and their suitability, any longer. Not when her sister Jane had still not recovered her happy nature from Mr. Bingley's abrupt departure and absence from Hertfordshire.

"Pardon me," she said, trying to keep her amusement at Miss Bingley's shocked countenance contained. "I cannot help admiring the fine instrument at the other end of the room."

She knew her boorish behavior should have concerned her, especially Mr. Darcy's opinion on the matter. But his estimation in her mind had fallen since their meeting yesterday. Elizabeth was unsure what her uncle and Mr. Darcy had discussed last evening. Still, undoubtedly, more than a weak apology to her should have been forthcoming.

Perhaps that was what he had been about to say to her before the Bingley sisters so rudely interrupted him in the foyer? But it was no matter; she walked to the piano and sat down to examine it.

Miss Bingley's voice reverberated behind her. "Miss Bennet is quite devoted to her studies. She perused books at Netherfield instead of playing cards or conversing with others in the room. Now she inspects a musical instrument instead of enjoying her host and his guests' company."

Elizabeth pounded a dissonant minor chord on the ivory keys. She was far enough removed that they could not discern her glare. She took a deep breath and then scrutinized the exquisite instrument before her. The keys responded quickly, none sticking like the piano at Longbourn. She could be very content practicing on this.

"Miss Bennet was an outstanding conversationalist yesterday. Please excuse me. She needs someone to turn the sheets for her."

Her fingers halted as she looked toward the far end of the sitting room, where Mr. Darcy was hastening towards her. She then glanced behind him to the Bingley sisters' stupefied features and bowed her head to obscure her smile.

CHAPTER 8

The piano, indeed, was a fine instrument. The keys responded to the lightest touch. Elizabeth could softly caress the keys to play the sheet music before her without it being loud enough for the gathering at the other end of the room to hear. Though she could listen to the notes in the air, the sound was not loud enough to drown out her pounding heartbeat as Mr. Darcy stopped next to the piano. He would be within her view if she raised her eyes from watching her fingers strike the keys.

"Miss Bennet."

Elizabeth let her fingers glide over the keys, playing another few measures of music while she composed her breathing. Surely he could not hear the pounding of her heart?

"Do you like the piano?"

She raised her head to see a grimace on his face that was quickly replaced by polite interest.

Slowly she answered, "It is an exquisite instrument."

Mr. Darcy shifted his stance and held his hands behind his back. He reminded her of Mr. Collins about to pontificate, except her cousin had never displayed any signs that he was nervous. "I would like to continue our conversation from earlier." He cleared his throat.

She frowned. He suddenly seemed more nervous. Surely Mr. Darcy was not, not here in front of—

"I am sure your uncle acquainted you with the nature of our discussion yesterday."

Elizabeth moved her hands off the piano and sat up straighter. This was not what she had expected to hear from him.

"I will travel to London to purchase a Special License tomorrow. We will be wed soon after I return."

Elizabeth blinked and closed her mouth, which she had not realized had dropped open. She curled her hands on her lap, her fingernails digging into her palms.

A frown appeared on Mr. Darcy's face. "Is something the matter?"

It was unfortunate he chose a public room for this. Elizabeth would have greatly relished being able to express herself freely. Instead, she had to control her features, so her feelings were not displayed to those watching from the room's far end. For she knew all of them had to be watching them. "Mr. Darcy, I know not what to say."

His frown grew more pronounced.

Elizabeth narrowed her eyes and tightened her fists. "Since I arrived at your estate the day before, I have been humiliated and embarrassed. I was tossed into the lake by your sheep, dressed in a maid's uniform with no maid to help me. Now you are not apologizing but have presumed to tell me how, when, and where we shall be married. And to think, you might have taken this chance to improve on the last proposal you made that I refused."

Mr. Darcy now stood stiffly, his hands by his side. "I had expected your uncle to share the details of our meeting yesterday. I apo—"

"A marriage contract was signed before you asked if I would accept your proposal?" Her voice trembled with anger.

Mr. Darcy hesitated before answering. "We were compromised, Miss Bennet."

"Yes, I am aware of that," Elizabeth said, eyes flashing. "But it is also customary for the man to at least ask the woman before they are betrothed."

He paused, and she wondered if he remembered the last time he had proposed. She only had the day before to ascertain if his behavior had improved to a more gentlemanlike manner, and yesterday at the lake, she would have answered in the affirmative. That answer changed when she was so abominably treated by his staff, no doubt at Mrs. Reynold's direction. And all he had apologized for thus far was for the sheep!

"Miss Elizabeth Bennet, will you do me the honor of becoming my wife?"

She stilled on the bench in front of the exquisite piano, taking in the beautifully appointed room. But material goods and money had never interested her. No, she sought love. Elizabeth had told her family and friends that she would only marry for true, deep, and abiding love.

And now she was compromised. To the man she had rejected only four months before. She grimaced at what she had said to him then, before she had read the letter he had written for her, divulging secrets regarding Mr. Wickham… then she shook her head, spying Miss Bingley looking directly at her. Elizabeth could not forget that Mr. Darcy had conspired against her sister, Jane, to keep her apart from the man she loved.

Elizabeth looked up at Mr. Darcy, who had stiffened with a blank face. It was apparent he was expecting to be rejected again. She wanted to spurn him just for yesterday's embarrassing treatment. For Jane's sake.

Still, his letter, delivered to her in Rosings park, helped her understand him much better. Her feelings towards him had undergone such a material change that she knew he was not a proud, arrogant man. Just misunderstood. After his sheep had knocked her into the lake, it appeared he still cared for her.

Would those sentiments, emotions she guessed he held, be enough to ensure a successful marriage? She sighed. There was nothing to consider; only one option remained, one that would protect her family's honor and her sister's chances of a good marriage.

"I agree."

His eyes lit, his features so transformed that she could only stare in amazement. Mr. Darcy smiling was a sight to behold. She felt a stirring in her chest, her breath quickening. She had never thought him ugly. No, he was always quite handsome, but his arrogant pride had always overshadowed his looks to her. But now... no, she would still not fall into this marriage just because of a sheep.

"I do have a request though, Mr. Darcy—"

"Please, call me Fitzwilliam."

Elizabeth blinked. They were betrothed, she had leave to call him by his name, but it had all happened so quickly. She still did not even know him well, this version of him, the more gentlemanly one. "I would like to be courted. Our marriage, I believe, would have a greater chance of being satisfactory to us both if we—"

"Miss Bennet!" Mr. Bingley rushed into the room with a young, tall, blonde girl on his arm. He stopped next to his sisters at the other end of the room.

Miss Bingley sourly glared down the room in their direction and made no move to introduce the Gardiners, who were on the settee on Mr. Bingley's other side.

"I had heard you were here." Mr. Bingley smiled at the Gardiners and then quizzically gazed at his eldest sister before turning in Elizabeth's direction. "Please forgive me; I would have come down right away had I—well, you are here, and I am happy to see you again!"

He looked down at his sister again, his smile greatly diminished. Miss Bingley studiously ignored him.

Elizabeth stood up and smoothed her skirts to hide her trembling hands. Truly she was astonished at how overcome with emotion she was. They were compromised; they had to wed. Why had her heart leaped when he had proposed?

She returned Mr. Darcy's smile, her heart fluttering. He bent his arm, she hesitated, then placed her hand on his in what felt like a momentous occasion. They strode to the other end of the sitting room. Elizabeth hoped none of her thoughts were displayed on her features; it was a failing she had worked to over-come. Still, on occasions of great emotion, she strug-gled with the task.

Mr. Bingley looked back and forth between Mr. Darcy and herself as they approached the grouping. "I can not tell you how delighted I was when Darcy informed me you were not five miles from Pember-ley. How do you do? I can see that you are well."

"Very well, indeed. Thank you."

"Good, excellent. And your family?"

"Very well, sir." An impish smile came to her lips. "Some of my family is here." She gestured to the settee where the Gardiners sat. "May I introduce them to you?"

Mr. Bingley's surprise was evident. The sting of his expectation that her relations would behave like her family hurt less than it would have last year before she had time to realize Mr. Darcy's criticism of her family was nothing she had not thought herself.

Introductions were made between the Gardiners and Mr. Bingley, who then said, "I shall allow Darcy to make the introductions of this fine young lady."

Elizabeth studied the pair. Why would he not introduce the woman he escorted into the room? She had thought them courting. But the girl left Mr. Bingley's side to stand near Mr. Darcy.

"May I introduce my sister, Miss Georgiana Darcy? Georgiana, this is Miss Elizabeth Bennet and her relatives, Mr. and Mrs. Gardiner."

Her eyes widened, but quickly Miss Darcy smiled and greeted her betrothed's younger sister. Georgiana was incredibly shy, not at all proud and arrogant as Mr. Wickham had wanted her to believe. Elizabeth looked between Mr. Bingley and Miss Darcy but saw no signs of matrimonial interest. Just natural affection, such as they were family friends. For Jane's sake, she hoped that was a correct supposition.

"Pray, tell me," stated Mr. Bingley. "Are all your sisters still at Longbourn?"

Elizabeth could not help the twitch of her lips. "All except one." He waited expectantly for her answer, which boosted her spirits. Mr. Bingley would not be this eager to hear her answer if he was engaged to anyone else. "My youngest sister is at Brighton."

"Ah. It seems too long…it is too long since I had the pleasure of speaking to you."

"It must be several months."

"It is above eight months at least. We have not met since the 26th of November when we danced together at Netherfield."

She could not even remember how long it had been, and it was telling that Mr. Bingley remembered the exact date he had last seen and danced with Jane.

"Do you know," said Mr. Bingley gazing off into the distance, "I do not think I can remember a happier time than those short months I spent in Hertfordshire."

"I hope, Bingley," proclaimed Mr. Darcy, "that you will be in residence in Hertfordshire again this fall in time for the holidays." His statement was met with puzzled looks from his friend and sister. "For my betrothed and I will be visiting relatives there."

Elizabeth glanced at Mr. Darcy to her right and clasped her skirts. This was not how she had expected him to inform those gathered. A movement from the sofa to her left, where the Bingley sisters sat, caught her attention. The Bingley sisters were sitting straight up, Miss Bingley pale and glaring at Mr. Darcy with barely concealed horror and hope. Elizabeth looked away, biting her bottom lip.

"Brother?" Georgiana looked up; the confusion was evident in her features.

Elizabeth sighed. She would need to ensure she was the one communicating any announcements in the future. Or at least guide him on how to do it without causing consternation in the listeners.

"May I present my betrothed, who has accepted my suit and made me the happiest of men."

Elizabeth tried to stop the blushing of her cheeks but failed miserably. She felt all eyes upon her. "Miss Elizabeth Bennet."

The shock on Mr. Bingley's face, and a quick glance to Georgiana showed the same, was disconcerting. But she could not blame their astonishment. She would have felt the same if a betrothal had been announced out of the blue without courting beforehand.

Mr. Bingley, now recovered, was the first to speak, his gaze repeatedly darting from her to Mr. Darcy. "Darcy! I...I congratulate you." His face filled with a smile at the happy news.

The men shook hands while Georgiana stood staring at Elizabeth, her eyes shining with excitement and happiness. "I have longed for a sister, Miss Bennet! And have heard so much about you from my brother."

"I can not imagine what he has said." Elizabeth was struck that he had talked of her to his sister, another sign of the depth of his affection. "Please, call me Elizabeth, for we are soon to be sisters."

The Gardiners approached, relief and joy filling them at the news. "I had thought he would propose immediately today," Mrs. Gardiner said quietly to Elizabeth, grasping her hand and pulling her niece into an embrace.

"I believe he was in the process earlier in the foyer when we were interrupted by Miss Bingley," Elizabeth admitted, her cheeks flushing pink with embarrassment.

Elizabeth glanced at the Bingley sisters standing by the fire, both looking petrified. Though Miss Bingley looked the worst, as if on the verge of swooning from horror. Elizabeth grinned.

CHAPTER 9

*M*r. Smythewick, a footman, employed for years at Pemberley and now a young man, strode into the doorway and declared that supper was served. Mr. Darcy's smile widened at the anticipation of the announcement that supper was ready. He had fantasized about walking into supper with Elizabeth Bennet on his arm since that first Assembly in Meryton. Until he heard the loud thud behind him.

He swiveled and stifled a groan, carefully containing his face. Mrs. Hurst remained speechless, staring at the crumpled heap. Miss Bingley had fainted dead away on the sitting room floor in front of the settee she had shared with her sister.

Elizabeth was the first to act. She quickly reached Miss Bingley, bending over and looking at her head. "I do not think she hit her head when she fell. Please." She now looked up at Mrs. Hurst, standing rigid next to the settee. "Could you pass me that pillow? I shall place it beneath her head."

"Caroline!" Mr. Bingley rushed to his sister's side, horrified at her sudden infirmity.

Mr. Darcy stepped forward, Elizabeth's voice having penetrated his shock at the display in front of him. She offered her assistance even though the woman had been unkind to Elizabeth. His contentment and warmth towards his betrothed expanded. Her generous nature was one reason he was so attracted to her. It reminded him of what little he recalled of his mother.

"I believe it best, Mr. Smythewick, to convey her to her room. I will have the doctor sent for." He motioned for the footman to approach as he yanked the bell.

At that pronouncement, Miss Bingley restored her senses. "Oh, oh my. What has happened?"

"Do not move, Caroline. You fainted." Mrs. Hurst threw a look at the approaching footman that immobilized him in his tracks. She turned to Mr. Darcy. "Do you have a sedan to carry her upstairs?"

"I am well, Louisa," Miss Bingley said, sitting up with her hand pressed to her forehead. "The surgeon does not need to be summoned. I will not be attending supper, though, Mr. Darcy. My apologies."

"Caroline, do not get up. You could injure yourself further!" cried her brother.

"Of course, Miss Bingley. However, I think it wise if you do not walk right away." Mr. Darcy shifted his gaze to the puzzled footman. "Fetch a chair, and two other men, then carry Miss Bingley to her room."

"There is no need for me to be taken in a sedan, Mr. Darcy," Miss Bingley said irritably as she extended a hand to him.

"Nonsense, you are unwell, and I would not want you dropping again." Mr. Darcy stepped back from the suddenly ill woman, disregarding her outstretched arm.

Three footmen entered the room with a light but sturdy chair, one of the armchairs from France that appeared out of place at Pemberley but would fit in nicely at Rosings.

"Honestly," exclaimed Miss Bingley, trying to rise again, "there is no requirement. I—"

"Caroline, you are sick, and care must be taken that you will not fall again." Mr. Bingley signaled the footmen to approach. "Please, they will safely bring you upstairs to rest."

After a brief glance around the room with a twitching eyelid, Miss Bingley allowed herself to be aided by the footman and settled in the chair. Which was scooped up and carried away by the footmen. Mrs. Hurst trailed them immediately.

"What?" Mr. Hurst snorted as he woke. "Come, come, supper is served. Well?"

Mr. Bingley grimaced. Did the man not even take note of his wife and sister-in-law having left the room? Mr. Darcy spun to face his betrothed, who exchanged a look with her aunt. He proffered his arm. "Elizabeth."

She grinned at him, but he noticed it was not as large or happy a smile that she distributed with her sisters or the Gardiners. But in time, he was optimistic they would have a prosperous marriage. Though his heart sank at the sight all the same.

He had difficulty focusing on the fine meal his Cook served, with Elizabeth sitting beside him. Georgiana was quiet, but Elizabeth drew her out with questions. Then his sister talked freely with Mr. Bingley and the Gardiners. Mr. Darcy was pleased; his sister was quite timid, and he tried to involve her in more social events. Still, as she was not yet out and he was often traveling, Georgiana had fewer opportunities to conquer her shyness than he wished. But with a wife as kind and skilled a conversationalist as Elizabeth, he hoped his sister would overcome her affliction before her debut next year.

The meal passed quickly, and the women quit to retire to the sitting room while cigars were offered along with the standard port. The space was tranquil; possibly, the other men were thinking of the meal. In Mr. Darcy's case, he was trying to decide how discourteous it would be to stand and suggest they join the ladies. Now that his dream was nearly fulfilled, Elizabeth as his wife, he did not want to be separated from her should she alter her mind. His face dropped as he remembered her demanding that she be courted. That would be simple to do, though, rides through the countryside listing the finest features of Pemberley and Derbyshire.

His mind happily concluded that the courting business was easily solved. He signaled the men it was time to join the ladies. Entering, he was satisfied to see his sister and Elizabeth close together, conversing. It was uncharitable of him, but he was glad the Bingley sisters were not in attendance. All the women in the room were cheerfully talking with each other, all smiles and kindness. Not a single spiteful word amongst them.

"I understand that you are fond of music and play excellently," said Elizabeth.

Georgiana looked down at her hands. "Oh, no, not play excellently. I mean…but I am very fond of music. I should dearly love to hear you play and sing. My brother has told me he has rarely heard anything that gave him more pleasure."

Mr. Darcy fidgeted where he stood in the doorway, not yet detected by the room's inhabitants.

Elizabeth smiled. "Well, you shall, but I warn you, your brother has greatly exaggerated my talents. No doubt for some mischievous reason of his own."

His cheerful mood diminished again.

"Oh, no. That could not be so. My brother never exaggerates. He always speaks the absolute truth." Why did Elizabeth arch her eyebrow at that statement? "Except that sometimes I think he is a little too benevolent to me."

He then entered the room, moving towards the two most essential females in his life.

"An ideal elder brother, then." Elizabeth beamed while Georgiana giggled. His heart plummeted with joy at the view.

"I do not recall hearing you sing before, Miss Bennet!" said Mr. Bingley. "I would love to hear you."

The others agreed, and though she protested it was feeble, she rose, asking Georgiana to flip the pages for her. He had never dreamed of kissing a sheep, but at that moment, he would have gladly kissed all of his unruly sheep for bringing Elizabeth to him. His heart threatened to burst at the spectacle of Elizabeth playing and singing with his sister next to her. Then she glanced at him, and the world halted.

CHAPTER 10

*H*umming, Elizabeth rolled curling papers in the hair framing her face and reached for the curling iron.

"Be careful, Lizzy!" exclaimed Mrs. Gardiner as she entered her niece's room. "You do not want to burn your hand before Mr. Darcy calls."

She met her aunt's eyes in the reflection of the small mirror in the Inn's room. "I apologize, aunt. I will refrain from scaring you again," Elizabeth said with a cheeky smile.

"You are cutting it close."

She continued to curl another strand of hair on a piece of paper. "My curls do not last long, so it is better to curl them immediately before I depart."

Mrs. Gardiner sat on the end of the bed. "I do like that color on you. It is one of my favorites of your dresses."

"Let us hope Mr. Darcy finds it pleasing as well. It is far better than the blanket I wore, and he still offered for me." She turned on the stool, her face serious. "Tell me, aunt, how much did uncle have to convince Mr. Darcy to offer for me?"

Her aunt hesitated, nonplussed. "Lizzy! You were compromised. Anyone knew that."

"You did not look happy when we arrived at Pemberley yesterday."

"Your uncle and I had expected him to talk to you immediately, and when it was obvious he had not, well, you could not expect us to be pleased."

"You could not expect him to not do his duty, aunt. He is a gentleman and prides himself on being the best gentleman he can."

"You know him better than we had expected, Lizzy."

At that statement, Elizabeth turned back to the mirror.

"Did he court you in Hertfordshire?"

Elizabeth laughed under her breath and then stood. "No, he most assuredly did not like me then. Well, he did not show it, at least. I had no idea. Indeed I thought he disliked me as much as I did him."

Mrs. Gardiner joined her near the door. "Oh, Lizzy." Her aunt's usual pleasant demeanor fell. "I had hoped you would marry for love, as you had always declared. But you seem to get along well?"

"I...we seem to understand each other better now." Elizabeth quickly opened the door and entered the hall where Mr. Gardiner was waiting for them. She did not want that avenue of conversation to continue. That would lead to her revealing his horrible declaration at Hunsford and the dreadful things she had said. The less anyone knew of that scene, the better.

They descended the staircase just as Mr. Darcy entered the Lambton Inn. Elizabeth's entire body flushed at the sight of her handsome betrothed. She took a deep breath as she descended the rest of the steps, better able to get control of herself. However, she had not forgotten that he had declared they would get married before discussing it or asking for her hand. Even with her reticence on the matter, Elizabeth knew she was very fortunate indeed that Mr. Darcy was a gentleman and would do what was required. But as she had told him the day before, she wanted their felicity in marriage not left to chance.

After exchanging greetings, Mr. Darcy escorted Elizabeth outside and handed her up in his barouche. The carriage was well appointed, the bench quite comfortable. But it was not as large as a coach, and her thigh brushed up against his when he shifted on the bench beside her.

Mr. Darcy must have instructed the driver beforehand on the intended route as he gave no instructions but pointed out the various features in Lambton and then amongst the Derbyshire countryside. Mrs. Gardiner and Mr. Darcy discussed their love of the large tree by the smithy and how they had climbed on it as children.

Elizabeth learned much about her betrothed during the ride and conversation with her aunt. It was still astonishing how more talkative he was in comparison to any other time she had met him. She could not determine if it was due to a determined change in his behavior or was it due to his being more comfortable in his own land.

They were now on the far northern end of his lands when Mr. Darcy called for the driver to stop, and they all descended to walk along the riverbank. Mr. Darcy indicated the best fishing spots to Mr. Gardiner and invited him to fish anytime he wanted at Pemberley.

Mrs. Gardiner leaned close to Elizabeth. "I shall never be quite happy till I have been all round the park. A low phaeton, with a nice little pair of ponies, would be the very thing."

Elizabeth glanced at Mr. Darcy to see that he was occupied in describing which outcropping of the bank concealed the biggest trout. Then she turned to her aunt. "I shall not request it too soon in the marriage for fear he thinks I am mercenary."

"Lizzy, no one who knows you would think that. You told me yourself how disagreeable he had been in Hertfordshire. You are the last person anyone would think had purposely tried to compromise him."

The two men then walked back to the barouche and continued their tour of the grounds of Pemberley. An open field not far from the stream was dotted with wildflowers and a large oak tree.

"What a perfect tableau. I could not think of a more perfect setting for outdoor luncheons and picnics." Elizabeth turned to her betrothed. "Do you have outdoor luncheons under the tree?"

"I have a faint memory of attending one as a child. I can easily arrange one if you would enjoy it?"

Elizabeth glanced away, the heady knowledge that this man would arrange matters to please her making her blush. She glanced at her aunt and saw excitement and wonder in her eyes. Her aunt would no doubt continue her line of questioning again that she was better acquainted with the man next to her than she had led them to believe. "I think that would be wonderful if it would not be too much of a bother."

"None at all. It is settled. I will call for you tomorrow for an outdoor luncheon."

The barouche turned back towards the village. Then, Mr. Darcy needed to take care of business matters he had neglected while away for several months.

Elizabeth was surprised at how much she wished they did not have to part.

THE NEXT DAY ARRIVED SLOWLY; such was Elizabeth's anticipation for the outdoor luncheon. At Longbourn, they had spread several blankets and lugged a basket of wrapped sandwiches for the meal. The last time they had attempted such a thing had been many years ago. Mrs. Bennet had detested the experience, and it had never been repeated. Except for the times Elizabeth roamed the paths through their land and nibbled an apple while perched on Oakham Mount.

She was sure whatever food would be in the basket Mr. Darcy would provide would be far superior, but it did not matter to her. An outdoor luncheon was an event she was predisposed to find utterly delightful.

When the barouche Mr. Darcy sent for Elizabeth and the Gardiners arrived at Pemberley, it was to a sight she could not have imagined in her wildest dreams. There were the expected large blankets on the grass. However, the tables and chairs on them were not. Nor were the table clothes, plates, glasses, covered dishes of food, vases of flowers, and footmen ready to serve. But that was not all, as croquet hoops were set up on the field awaiting players. Elizabeth closed her mouth thankfully before the barouche stopped, and Mr. Darcy took her hand to assist her descent.

"I hope you approve?"

Elizabeth could not take her eyes from the picnic, no, outdoor luncheon set before her. "How could I not? It is…it is remarkable."

She turned to him, a grin on her features. Then she saw her favorite childhood game on the field by the blankets, hoops, and sticks. Had her aunt mentioned it to him yesterday? Elizabeth glanced at Mrs. Gardiner but found her praising the foresight to have vases with flowers on the corners of the blankets.

How long had this taken his staff to arrange and prepare? This, indeed, could not have been undertaken by a smaller estate. Elizabeth felt honored and was struck by the wealth and power Mr. Darcy commanded. Even though she had never chased men for their prestige and wealth, she could understand its appeal.

He bent his arm and escorted her to the table as another equipage approached bearing the rest of the party. The youngest Bingley sister seemed to have recovered from her fainting spell the day before, though not as lively. The news of Mr. Darcy's betrothal must still be affecting her.

Once they were seated, covers were removed from the dishes, and the actual fare was revealed. The expected finger sandwiches, slices of ham, and cheese were present and accompanied by the unexpected—bottles of wine, a variety of pies, and freshly caught trout. The trout melted on her tongue.

"This is exquisite, Mr. Darcy," stated her uncle. "From your stream?"

"Yes. I could not regale you with my fishing tales the day before without snagging our luncheon this morning." Mr. Darcy answered Mr. Gardiner while he stared at Elizabeth.

Elizabeth could scarcely concentrate on her meal. She had asked him to court her, and he was doing an exemplary job. When they had some semblance of privacy, she would tell him so. Perhaps during croquet. Or during a walk by the stream.

With the feast concluded, the pies were covered but stayed on the table for the time being. The group approached the croquet hoops, even Miss Bingley. Elizabeth was unsure what surprised her more regarding Miss Bingley. That she deigned to join in playing a children's game or her display of not inconsiderable skill at thumping her ball through the hoops.

When Georgiana and Elizabeth were stuck at the same hoop, they reached an agreement. "Your brother is quite good at croquet. It would be a shame if my poor aim knocked his ball far out of play."

A shocked glance preceded Georgiana's giggles. They both aimed their balls and slammed Mr. Darcy's far from the next hoop. He did not mind, though. He was ever the perfect gentleman, happy that everyone was enjoying themselves.

"This was a splendid idea, Darcy!" exclaimed Mr. Bingley. "I have never enjoyed myself more."

"I should not be the recipient of your praise, Bingley. That honor goes to Miss Bennet, for a picnic was her proposal."

The Gardiners agreed it had been an excellent scheme, their happiness and delight evident. Mrs. Hurst declared it was a pleasant diversion, but Miss Bingley was silent and looked ill. Mr. Hurst had not joined his wife in the game. He was face down on the table, exuding intermittent snorts.

After the game of croquet concluded, Georgiana and Elizabeth proclaimed themselves the winners for slamming Mr. Darcy's ball away from every hoop he attempted to capture. Mr. Bingley was a surprisingly good shot but conceded that the ladies won as they did a respectable job of taking care of his main competitor, Mr. Darcy.

Georgiana and Elizabeth walked back to the picnic table arm in arm, laughing. The table had been set up perfectly, as it was now entirely in the shade of the big oak tree.

They all resumed their seats for pudding, with the expected pies now including tarts. Elizabeth had difficulty choosing between a custard and an apple tart. She could not remember an entire afternoon she had been so pleasantly entertained.

"Miss Bennet," asked Georgiana. "Have you played hoops and sticks?"

"It was my favorite game as a child. I have not played in some time. Shall we play now?"

The pair finished their individual tarts and then strode out from under the shade into the sun, where the hoops and sticks lay on the lawn. They each took turns gripping the stick, with the other hurling the hoops to land them on the stick. Much laughter ensued as it was a game Elizabeth loved, but she was notoriously horrendous at it. She could even hear her aunt laughing at her and then screaming.

Wait, that was not right. Elizabeth pivoted to face the picnic. At first, she could not fathom what was causing distress, but then Miss Bingley stood yanking at her dress and shrieking.

"Beast! Help! This foul beast is eating my dress by Madame Devy!"

Elizabeth sprinted back to the picnic as the gentlemen, apart from Mr. Hurst, rose to aid Miss Bingley. As she rounded the table to the far side and the screaming woman, she stopped and hurriedly clamped her hand over her mouth. Laughter would not be tolerable at this moment. Miss Bingley's costly dress of gold-threaded muslin was in the jaws of a sheep.

"Abominable creature! Where did it come from?"

The creature in question tossed its head, the thunderous rip of Miss Bingley's dress reverberating through the air. Along with a long, drawn-out scream.

The men moved immediately while Mrs. Hurst bellowed at the footmen to do something. Miss Bingley held her hands over the exposed shift on her right leg. Mr. Darcy captured and steadied the sheep by the wool around its neck as the beast devoured its stolen feast. Mrs. Gardiner approached and offered her wrap, which Mr. Bingley secured around his sister's waist. It mainly covered the sizeable missing piece of her expensive dress.

"Sheep! I loathe sheep! Dirty, filthy—"

"Caroline!" Mr. Bingley clutched the crying woman's arm. He guided her to their barouche, which had just arrived from whence it had waited for the picnic's conclusion further down the field.

"What? Abominable nuisance, eating out of doors." Mr. Hurst snorted loudly, raising his head from where it had lain next to his pudding.

His wife seized his arm, and they entered the barouche accompanying the still howling Miss Bingley. At the same time, her brother attempted unsuccessfully to soothe her. The lamenting and the hoofbeats diminished into the distance, and the ensuing peace and quiet was a welcome respite.

The sheep, who had concluded the feast, lifted her head to identify the next source of nourishment dangling off the table just a few steps away. The clashing of dishes as the tablecloth was abruptly snatched by the sheep's strong teeth accompanied the utensils scattered about onto the blanket underneath.

Cries of alarm and gasps filled the air. Mr. Darcy rapidly reached the peckish ewe, and with the help of Mr. Gardiner and two footmen, they blocked the rest of the tablecloth from becoming fodder for the voracious beast. However, the damage was done and shattered china littered the blanket at the sheep's feet.

"She is formidably strong!" exclaimed Mr. Gardiner as he watched the two footmen push against the sheep to restrain her from charging forward for another bite of the tablecloth.

"Yes. Excellent Derbyshire stock," said Mr. Darcy dryly.

Elizabeth muffled her mouth as a laugh threatened to escape. But the absurdity of what had just occurred would not leave her. She turned her back to conceal her struggles, tears streaming from her eyes at the effort.

"Oh, Miss Bennet, please do not cry." Georgiana stood next to her, anxiety and concern plainly etched on her features.

Struggling to speak in between stifling her laughter, "Georgiana…no, I… apologies…for…giving the… wrong…impression. I am…trying…to contain…my laughter!" And then she could talk no more, for she had utterly failed at the endeavor and could barely stand as she bent over at the waist, her shoulders shaking with mirth.

Giggles joined in from Georgiana, then the rest of the party participated in the laughter, which as a rule, is quite contagious.

A young sheepherder ran down the field and then stopped as the destruction the beast had caused became evident. The young lad was waved forward by Mr. Darcy, who surrendered the beast to his care.

"How did it stray off this far from the herd?"

The lad appeared to be almost in tears, fear of losing his post obvious. "This one is always causing trouble, sir."

"Have no worries. You are not losing your position. And your pay will not be docked." He looked at Elizabeth with a twinkle in his eye. "This creature is the cause of my future bliss, and I shall not hold her misbehavior against you."

The lad reacted by dipping his head, a huge smile gracing his dirty face.

"I would like her kept in the small fenced field next to the stables," ordered Mr. Darcy. "The beast will be less likely to flee and cause trouble then."

The sheepherder bowed and escorted the cantankerous creature toward the stables near the house.

With the picnic ended, footmen tidied up the mess and packed the dishes, and their carriage was called forth. Mr. Darcy handed Elizabeth into the barouche.

As they slowly drove away, Elizabeth continued to look behind her, committing the scene of Mr. Darcy standing in front of the outdoor luncheon to memory. She did not want to forget when she fell in love with Mr. Darcy.

CHAPTER 11

The next day after luncheon at the Lambton Inn, the Gardiners and Elizabeth rose from the table. The maid entered the room, holding letters. "If you please, ma'am. The Post's just come."

Elizabeth seized the Post. "Two letters from Jane. At last! I wondered why we had not heard anything."

She tried not to show her excitement that she had an excuse to avoid the outing. "Would you be very angry if I requested to postpone our outing? I shall remain here and read my letters."

"Not at all," replied Mrs. Gardiner. "Of course, you want to read your letters. Your uncle and I will visit my friend and return for you in an hour."

The Gardiners departed, and Elizabeth settled on the sofa on the other side of the private sitting room, unfolding the first letter from Jane. It was a pleasant letter describing the Gardiner children and the nice weather. She also wrote that Kitty had just stopped crying, having not been invited to Brighton like Lydia had. Mrs. Bennet had finally ceased mentioning the cruelty of not allowing both sisters to go.

Elizabeth sighed, glad that she was far removed from that situation. And that Mrs. Bennet was far removed from her. She knew that if her mother had been there, she would have been beside herself with the news that her second eldest would marry the man with £10,000 a year. Elizabeth was immensely relieved her family was far away from Derbyshire.

She put that letter aside and picked up the second, which was also from Jane but had been addressed quite poorly, almost entirely illegible. How odd, it did not look as if the rain had washed the address away but that Jane herself had written it with a shaky hand. With misgivings, Elizabeth unfolded the letter.

*"Dearest Lizzy, since writing my last letter, something
has occurred of a most unexpected and serious nature,
but I am afraid of alarming you. Be assured we are all
well. What I have to say relates to poor Lydia."*

"Lydia?!" exclaimed Elizabeth.

*"An express arrived at twelve last night, just as we were
all gone to bed. The letter was from Colonel Forster to
inform us that Lydia was gone off to Scotland with one
of his officers. To confess the truth, with Wickham. You
will understand our surprise and shock. To Kitty,
however, it does not seem so entirely unexpected. We are
certain they are heading to Gretna Green, though
perhaps through London first. Lydia has always wanted
to go to London."*

Then in even worse handwriting, more was added to
the already shocking news.

*"We have received more news and I warn you, Lizzy, it
is not good. Lydia has arrived at Meryton on the Post
coach. Wickham had deserted her—"*

"Oh no!"

"—at a Post stop. They were to take the Post coach to London. Still, while using the facilities, Wickham took the coach heading north, according to passersby. I can not credit Wickham acting in such a manner, and I am not sure this is an accurate retelling of events."

"I can! Just after he destroyed the reputation of Lydia, how could you not trust it?"

"Thankfully, Lydia was lent the fare to Meryton, but she arrived unaccompanied. I fear she did not keep her sentiments regarding Wickham to herself on the journey."

"Oh, Lydia! How could you?"

"Colonel Forster states that they are attempting to locate Wickham. Thankfully they are spreading the report that Wickham and Lydia are engaged. That should help safeguard her reputation until they find him and they are married. Oh, Lizzy, how I wish you were here, as Mama is in hysterics. Kitty has been banished to her bedroom until Papa is no longer angry with her. I do wish you would come back quickly. Mr. Gardiner would be of great aid to calm Mama and aid in the search for Wickham. Dearest Lizzy, I cannot

refrain from begging you all to come here as soon as possible."

Elizabeth stood and paced the room, still clutching the letters in her hand. She had implored Mr. Bennet against allowing Lydia to accompany Colonel Forster's wife, who was only one year older than Lydia, to Brighton. How imprudent of her to divulge her grievances regarding Wickham on the Post coach. Hopefully, the passengers would remember that they were already married and not just betrothed.

What would need to be done before they could depart for Hertfordshire? She halted in her traverse around the room. Would Mr. Darcy want to marry her with Wickham, soon to be his brother-in-law?

Then the maid opened the door. "If you please, ma'am."

In walked Mr. Darcy. "Miss Bennet, I hope this…."

"I beg your pardon. I must locate Mr. Gardiner on business that cannot wait." Elizabeth was stunned, staring at the man she loved with trepidation because of what she knew would happen once she told him the news.

"Good God, what is the matter?"

Elizabeth sniffed.

"Of course, I will not detain you for a moment, but let me go or send a servant to fetch Mr. and Mrs. Gardiner. You are unwell. You cannot go yourself."

Mr. Darcy took her arm, guided her to a chair, and then sat down across from her, taking her hand. "You are unwell. May I call a doctor?"

"No, I am well." She stared at the letters in her hands.

"Is there nothing you can take for your present relief? A glass of wine? Truly, you look very ill."

She sniffed again and dabbed her eyes with a hand-kerchief. "No, I thank you. There is nothing wrong with me. I am quite well. I am only distressed by some awful news I have just received from Longbourn."

Her voice cracked, and Elizabeth dropped her head, trying to restore her composure. Mr. Darcy brought his fist to his mouth, still gripping her hand.

"I am sorry, forgive me. I have just received a letter from Jane, with such horrendous news it cannot be concealed from anyone. You shall not be surprised with what you know of the man. My youngest sister, Lydia, has abandoned all her friends and has eloped with Mr. Wickham. They have fled together from Brighton. You know him too well to doubt the rest. But it is even worse—" She stifled a sob. "He deserted her at a Post stop. She arrived in Meryton alone."

Mr. Darcy stood abruptly and walked to the fireplace rubbing his hands on his face.

"She has no money, no connections, nothing to attract him. My parents are sharing the news with everyone that the couple is wed, and Wickham had to return north."

Elizabeth released her breath and suddenly felt exhausted. It should not have amazed her that Mr. Darcy stood to move away from her. Her dread grew that he would call off their engagement no matter how the news would affect his reputation. But that did not signify now. Not when she and her family's reputation was ruined due to Lydia's heedlessness.

"Your words to me last year were astute," said Elizabeth.

Mr. Darcy spun towards her, his hands held behind his back. "Please, let us not speak of what I said then. It does not portray me in the best light."

They were both quiet, except for Elizabeth's sniffs. She was sure that no matter how kind a man she now knew Mr. Darcy was, her betrothal to the man she loved was over.

"I am afraid you have long been desiring my absence. This unfortunate incident will, I fear, prevent my sister's having the pleasure of seeing you at Pemberley today."

"Oh, yes. Be so kind as to apologize for us. Say that crucial business calls us home immediately. And if you would be so kind as to conceal the sad truth as long as possible."

"You may be assured of my secrecy. But I have stayed too long." He lifted his hat and riding stick. "I shall leave you now."

Elizabeth stood, still grasping the letters that sealed her family's fate. Mr. Darcy stared into her eyes as if memorizing her features, then quit the room. She hastily turned away, letting the tears fall until the door opened again.

Spinning around with hope in her heart, it plummeted to dread when her aunt and uncle stepped into the room, ready for their outing that afternoon. Elizabeth despised being the bearer of bad news. Still, in this case, there was no one else to do the job, and urgency precluded her from prolonging the pain.

After her aunt and uncle recovered from their shock and misery, Mrs. Gardiner said, "Even if what you say of Wickham is true, I still cannot credit this of Lydia."

"Ever since the militia were quartered at Meryton, there has been nothing but love, flirting, and officers in her brain!" Elizabeth wiped her cheek.

"If he can be found expeditiously," interjected Mr. Gardiner, "then a marriage between him and Lydia will take place, and the worst will be evaded."

Elizabeth's uncle had a disposition that believed anything would resolve satisfactorily. This was advantageous for a shop owner of an import business but not so practical when it came to his niece running away with a man who had unilaterally abandoned her.

"We must not assume the worst," declared Mrs. Gardiner. Elizabeth shook her head. "It is probable, Lizzy."

"Indeed it is," agreed Mr. Gardiner. "Why would any young man form a plan against a girl who is by no means unprotected or friendless?"

Elizabeth took a deep breath and stayed quiet. They were not cognizant of all the details regarding Wickham that she was. And she felt it was partially her fault for not disclosing his character once she knew the truth. But that would have betrayed Mr. Darcy's confidence and besmirched the reputation of his younger sister. Which she would never do, and so again, she concluded that there had been nothing she could have done to stop this that she had not already attempted.

She followed her aunt and uncle out of the private room into the hallway. Mr. and Mrs. Gardiner stopped abruptly, and Elizabeth almost collided with them. She peered around her uncle and saw someone had walked out of the servant's door. Mr. Wickham.

Both parties were dumbstruck. Elizabeth still clasped the letters delivering Jane's dreadful news in her hands. Wickham must have accompanied those very letters on the Post coach.

"Mr. Wickham!" She stepped around the Gardiners while endeavoring not to let any of her thoughts show on her face. She did not know how, but they had to keep Wickham in their sights and alert her family.

The man grinned and bowed with every appearance of a well-bred gentleman. "Miss Bennet, how unexpected to see you here. And these are your relatives. I remember them from your aunt's card party in Meryton."

"Yes, we are sightseeing in the Peak District on holiday."

"I had never imagined you to travel to Derbyshire. As I recall, you had mentioned you wanted to avoid a certain someone."

Elizabeth was careful not to give any signal that she was vexed and would rather slap him across the face than play nice. But to preserve her family's reputation and forcibly keep Wickham until her family could arrive to demand a marriage, she would act to the best of her ability. "My aunt and uncle invited me to accompany them on their tour. I could not reject a chance to view a part of England I had heard so much about."

Then she realized those very letters detailing Wickham's misdeeds were in her hands, in full view of the reprobate himself. She pulled her hands behind her back with what she hoped was a natural movement. "We have been enjoying a wonderful time viewing the peaks and where my aunt spent her childhood. You spent your formative years in Derbyshire as well, did you not?"

Elizabeth felt the letters dragged out of her hands. Mrs. Gardiner most likely, and hopefully, could obscure them in her reticule without catching Wickham's notice.

"I did indeed. I spent my childhood like a son to the late Mr. Darcy, the most generous of men. It is a pity his son has not turned out with the same benevolent nature."

"Have you also returned to visit your friends and family?" asked Mrs. Gardiner.

"I am very fond of this village, and with a short respite from the militia, I chose to visit my friends and family here."

Mr. Gardiner cleared his throat. "Would you care to join us in our private dining room? It is good to greet an old friend from Hertfordshire."

Observing Wickham's face, she saw his eyes dart away to the outside door. He was on the edge of running, and they would likely never find him again. And her family's reputation would forever be sullied. "You must be parched after your travels."

Thankfully her uncle was a shrewd man. "Indeed, you must sit with us. I will buy the first round."

And with that, Wickham professed delight in spending time with old acquaintances from the country. Mrs. Gardiner and Elizabeth followed the men back into the room, exchanging wide-eyed glances but not uttering a word of their thoughts.

As she sat and smiled sweetly at Wickham, her thoughts were filled with the quandary of how they would keep Wickham in Lambton until her family could arrive. If they dispatched a letter by an express rider, it would reach Longbourn in less than twelve hours. But for Lydia and Mr. Bennet to travel north would take a sennight, at least. She could not think of any method that did not involve the scoundrel held in the local gaol.

The two men continued to exchange tales of travel and excellent locations in Derbyshire. At the same time, Mr. Gardiner regularly provided Wickham with drinks. Elizabeth was suspicious of her uncle when he showed no signs of overindulgence, yet Wickham was swaying in his seat.

"I imagine you are quite fatigued," stated Mr. Gardiner. "You had just arrived on the Post coach today?"

Mr. Wickham started to nod but then frowned. Elizabeth's heart raced, and she flicked her eyes at her uncle.

Mr. Gardiner continued, "We are going to sightsee the church and then call upon old friends, but we have a set of rooms upstairs. Why do you not rest, and we will call back for supper?"

Elizabeth stared at her uncle, hoping her shock was not evident in her features.

"Much obliged. I am…shall accept your offer."

Mr. Gardiner stood, but Wickham needed help to remain upright. Elizabeth turned away from the scene, her wrist caught by her aunt. "Come," the older woman whispered. "Let us go to our chambers and let your uncle be seen alone with Wickham."

A man's reputation could survive being seen assisting another man who had too much drink. Elizabeth hastily climbed the staircase, unsure how Mr. Gardiner had achieved this feat. But uppermost on her mind was how would they maintain the scoundrel for a sennight until her family could arrive? Would anyone miss him? And how would they keep Wickham's kidnapping secret?

She had a chance to ask her questions when her aunt followed her into Elizabeth's room. "What is uncle doing? How is he not appearing to show signs of drink? He had as much to drink as Wickham! We cannot—"

"Lizzy dear, come away from the door. We do not want to be overheard." Elizabeth walked to the far side of the chamber and sat on the bed while Mrs. Gardiner perched on the wooden chair in the corner. "Your uncle has a stratagem for those he must meet as part of his business but does not want to suffer for it. He pours it into the nearest plant."

Elizabeth gasped, then muffled her laughter.

"I did wonder how he showed no adverse effects. That is clever of him. But aunt, we will not be able to keep Wickham in our chamber. It will take a sennight at least for a letter to arrive and them to travel here!"

"Your uncle has had to confront unsavory situations a few times during his import business. I am sure he has a plan." Heavy steps sounded in the hallway as if someone was striding slowly and staggering.

She nearly suspended her breath, hoping Wickham would not perceive he had been tricked and would raise an outcry. But who would believe a gentleman had supplied a man with drink for a ploy?

CHAPTER 12

*D*arcy had galloped to Pemberley when he reached the turn that led up to his house. He reined in his horse, Caesar, and turned around to look back toward where he had come. It had taken that long for him to process what she had said about Wickham. That man had reared his ugly head in his affairs again.

He had thought he was rid of the man after thwarting the elopement of Georgiana with the scoundrel. The elopement he blamed entirely on Wickham manipulating the emotions of a younger girl. But then the man cropped up in Meryton, a small village at the other end of England from Derbyshire. And now, the reprobate had fled with

Elizabeth's youngest sister and immediately abandoned her.

Mr. Darcy groaned as he wheeled Caesar around
and jabbed him back the way they had just come.
Would he ever be free of that wastrel? No, it did not
seem likely he would be free of the man. As soon as
Mr. Darcy located him, he would compel Wickham
to marry Lydia, restoring her family's reputation.
Not for any sense of altruism for Lydia, who was one
of the reasons he had been set against ever marrying
Elizabeth. The other reason was her parents. No, he
was thinking only of his betrothed.

Which was why he was riding back to Lambton. For
in his haste to hunt down the wretch, he had
forgotten there was someone well acquainted with
Wickham still living on the outskirts of the village.
And there was only one reason the man would have
returned, and that was for money or revenge. Even
better, according to Wickham, if the two were
combined.

Which begged the question, how had word of his
engagement to Elizabeth Bennet reached Wickham?
He hoped that was not the cause of Wickham's
appearance in Lambton, but why else had the man
traveled back to Derbyshire? Mr. Darcy spurred his

horse faster. He needed to find the man before Wickham renewed his acquaintance with Elizabeth.

Having reached Lambton, Mr. Darcy guided his horse to the far edge of the village where Wickham's mother still resided in a small house. When the late Mr. Wickham was alive, the house had been dilapidated as the man had done nothing but drink while employed as the late Mr. Darcy's steward. After the elder Wickham passed, with George Wickham, a favorite of the late Mr. Darcy, Fitzwilliam's father paid for repairs on the Wickham home and provided food and comforts. After his father passed, Mr. Darcy saw no reason not to continue the practice. It was not Mrs. Wickham's fault that her husband was a drunkard and her son a worthless scoundrel.

Therefore the woman was well disposed to welcome Mr. Darcy when he jumped off Caesar and pounded on the door. After some time, just as he raised his hand to knock again, the door opened, revealing a hump-backed crone.

"Good day, madam. Would you know the location of your son's current whereabouts?"

She squinted, then her face brightened. "Mr. Darcy! How kind of you to visit. It has been some time since

I saw you last. Come in, come in, mighty fine tea I have and some biscuits too. I swept just yesterday—"

"Thank you, but I must decline. I am here on urgent business." Some guilt settled upon him for the untruth he would tell, but he knew there was no faster method to ascertain the son's whereabouts. "My solicitor has recently discovered a misplaced account at the bank meant for your son. There is a deadline before which the account must be turned over to its owner, or it will be lost."

"Blunt, you say? That is fortunate indeed! Yes, my son would greatly appreciate hearing that an account for him was found. Set up by your father, I 'spect, such a good man, your father. He loved my Georgie like a son. It was all Georgie spoke about Mr. Darcy this, Mr. Darcy that—"

"Yes, Mrs. Wickham. Have you heard from your son?" Mr. Darcy shifted his stance, eager to be on his way.

"My Georgie is coming home! I have not seen him in such a long time. He wrote me you see, for a place to stay while he visited friends in the area. Come home to his mum, he will. Such a good boy, many people fond of him as they should be."

Mr. Darcy could hardly believe his luck. He would not have to travel to London to find the man and would also be able to stay near Elizabeth and continue to court her. "When is he expected? I will have a solicitor on hand to witness the signing over of the account."

"Oh, not long, I think. You know how the Post is. The roads change with the weather."

Caesar whinnied and tossed his head up, sensing his master's impatience. "You are waiting for word from him about when he will arrive?"

The old woman cackled, showing her rotten yellow teeth. "Oh no, he is arriving today! On the Post, he is. He should be in town already, I expect. Taking time to make his way home to his mum as he always does. I 'spect he is at the pub where Molly is a maid. He still has a fondness for her, his first love."

He twitched at the shocking news, startling his horse, who stepped back and snorted. "Thank you very much, Mrs. Wickham. Good day."

Mr. Darcy jumped back on his horse, steered him towards the village proper, and jabbed him into a fast trot. Caesar could not move any faster due to the street's usual congestion. But the urgency that had consumed him exploded into an inferno as Wickham was in this same village. And soon to be found...at the pub at Lambton Inn. At the very same inn, Elizabeth was currently residing.

He spurred Caesar to a canter, but it seemed every villager in the county was conducting business in Lambton that afternoon. And everyone called out to him or bowed, requiring him to nod and touch his beaver hat, making what should have been a short trip prodigiously vexing at its length.

Eventually, they turned the corner. Mr. Darcy yanked Caesar to a stop in front of the white Tudor building and leaped down, tossing the reins to a stable lad. He strode into the Inn, spying a serving girl and a maid. Which one was Wickham's love? Before he could approach one, the Inn's proprietor accosted him.

"Mr. Darcy, how thankful I am for you to grace my fine establishment with your presence." The rotund man wiped his hands on a towel and then quickly tucked it away.

"Yes, I am hoping to find an acquaintance of mine, Mr. Wickham. I believe he was expected today on the Post coach. I heard he would stop here, and I have news for him."

The short man nodded. "Oh, Wickham, yes, yes, he did come to see Molly, but I believe he departed just as fast."

Mr. Darcy compressed his lips. The scoundrel was as slippery as an eel. He thanked the innkeeper for his knowledge, then whirled to walk back to the entrance when he stopped and signaled the young maid eagerly watching the discussion.

She hurriedly approached, her blonde braids swinging at her haste. "Yes, sir?"

"Have the Gardiners and Miss Bennet departed for Hertfordshire yet?"

"No, I have not heard they were departing today."

Mr. Darcy frowned at the news, which was quite unusual for people leaving in haste. At the least, orders should have been received for their carriage to be readied and pulled around. "Please tell Miss Bennet that Mr. Darcy is here to call upon her."

The girl curtsied and swiftly darted up the staircase while Mr. Darcy entered the private sitting room. He hoped she and the Gardiners had not left for

Hertfordshire already. Curse Wickham for fouling everything, including his own courting of Elizabeth.

The door opened behind him. Mr. Darcy spun to greet Elizabeth; instead, it was her uncle, alone.

"Good day, Mr. Darcy. My niece is, er, upstairs." The man fidgeted with the edge of his waistcoat.

Mr. Darcy narrowed his eyes. Something was wrong. "Has she taken ill?"

Or had Wickham already found her and was currently holding her at ransom? His heart thudded, and he clenched his fists.

Mr. Gardiner cleared his throat. "It would be best if I show you. Please, follow me."

With dread, Mr. Darcy frowned as he followed the man up the stairs to the small rooms for let. He could not concoct any scenario that could not be explained but needed to be witnessed.

Still, when Mr. Gardiner opened the door to the room, Mr. Darcy was not expecting the scene that had met him. Wickham was tied to a wooden chair, with a shawl tied across his mouth, looking dazed and confused.

Never had Mr. Darcy been so shocked, not even when his blasted sheep had catapulted Elizabeth into the pond. He regained control after closing his mouth and surveyed the room. In the corner, he spotted Elizabeth with her aunt. She looked abashed, yet she was also battling amusement as she returned his gaze.

Mr. Darcy marched into the room. "I believe an explanation is in order." He turned to Mr. Gardiner. "How did you manage to subdue him so quickly? I just learned he was expected on the Post today."

The tale was quickly revealed by Mr. Gardiner. If it had been anyone else, Mr. Darcy would have firmly believed the man was telling a great fib. Yet, he knew none in the room, save the scoundrel tied up on the chair, would think to tell a falsehood.

"You are to be commended for your quick thinking. An enticement such as that is not one Wickham would ignore."

Mr. Gardiner waved a hand toward his niece. "I must give credit where it is due. It was not my idea, but Elizabeth's."

An arched eyebrow over a pair of fine eyes greeted his astonished expression. He did not know whether

to be proud of his betrothed's quick wits or to repri-
mand her for putting herself in harm's way.
Wickham was known to be a dangerous man when
cornered. Since Mr. Darcy was not yet married to
the woman of his dreams, he chose the safest course
of action: to say nothing.

Instead, he faced the scoundrel sitting in the center
of the room, which during this entire time, had been
making muffled noises and trying to tug his arms
free.

CHAPTER 13

*E*lizabeth could not restrain her fidgeting, which would typically have drawn a response from her aunt. Still, it went to show the extraordinary circumstances as Mrs. Gardiner did not admonish her. Not even when she jumped from her perch on the edge of her bed to pace the small room. It was so small that her route consisted of four steps to the left, turn, four steps back, turn. At one point, she stopped and cocked her head to listen, but the voices in the Gardiners' room next door were muffled, and she could not make out any words. With a sigh, Elizabeth turned and repeated her route again.

Though she could not decipher Wickham's words, she could hear a loud yelp after a bang. Elizabeth

stilled and turned to her aunt, who shared her horrified expression. She could not envision either of the
men, her uncle or Mr. Darcy, to be the type to
pummel a man to gain their way. Wickham had most
likely just tumbled over in the chair. But why would
he have toppled over, except to escape a flying fist?

She gnawed her bottom lip and sat back down on
the edge of her bed next to Mrs. Gardiner. After
fretting over the noises' implications, Elizabeth
broached the subject with her aunt.

A perfunctory knock had Elizabeth whirl her head
to the door, which was opened by Mr. Gardiner.
"Please come to our sitting room. We have news."

It was quiet as they traversed the worn hallway with
its creaking boards. And still, no one spoke as they
descended the staircase, the banister worn by generations of hands rubbing it. Had the number of steps
doubled? Never could she remember waiting with
such breathless anticipation before. Except maybe
for a Christmas holiday when she was younger.
Much younger.

Finally, they were all in the small room, and Mr.
Darcy turned towards them after shutting the door
to the private sitting room.

"Mr. Gardiner, do not keep us in suspense any longer. What have you learned from that horrible man?" Mrs. Gardiner wrung her hands, a movement Elizabeth could not recall having seen her do before.

Mr. Gardiner sighed and massaged his face. "It pains me to inform you, but he had no intention of marrying Lydia."

Both women sunk onto the nearest chairs. Elizabeth closed her eyes but then pinned her uncle with a stare. "Did he have any explanation for his actions?"

Her uncle shook his head and beckoned the younger man standing near him. "He stated that the militia life did not agree with him. Quitting and leaving alone did not seem as thrilling as finding a companion to join him on his travels."

Elizabeth pursed her lips.

"He had every intention of meeting his friends in the North, if he had any still left, to assist in procuring new employment."

Mr. Darcy nodded to the women. "What he had told you was truthful, but traveling with Lydia was not what he had expected, and he deserted your sister."

Mrs. Gardiner finally spoke. "We are fortunate nothing untoward occurred during her travel to Hertfordshire."

"We are indeed," Mr. Gardiner exclaimed. "For abandoning her alone, I want to see that man flogged."

Her jaw dropped. Elizabeth had never heard her uncle speak in such severe terms. But that did not signify that she did not wholeheartedly agree with the sentiments. She wondered if Lydia knew how fortunate she had been that she had not been abducted and taken to London for nefarious purposes. Or accosted at the post stop with no funds, bags, or companion.

"Did he express any remorse whatsoever?"

Mr. Darcy lowered his eyes at Elizabeth's question while Mr. Gardiner sighed and shook his head. Elizabeth leaned back against the sofa with a huff.

The crackling of the fire was loud in the silence. It was not surprising, yet still shocking a man that had all semblance of a gentleman could behave in such a deplorable manner towards a young woman. Especially when he also expressed no thoughts of remorse.

"I will write directly to my brother-in-law and sister and send the news. No need to prolong their agony," said Mr. Gardiner.

Mr. Darcy nodded, muttered a hasty valediction, and hastened from the room without a glance at any of the other room's inhabitants, including Elizabeth. She quietly followed her aunt and uncle back up the staircase while turning over her betrothed's behavior in her mind. The shocking situation with Wickham had preoccupied her, but she did not think she had slighted him in any manner.

The only conclusion she could draw that had any logic was that he thoroughly regretted they were betrothed now that Wickham would be his brother-in-law. Elizabeth bit her bottom lip, then raised her head and swept into her room. What was done was done, and she would not spend any time pondering the thoughts and behavior of Mr. Darcy.

She ignored the sour feeling in her chest as she wrote Jane to share particulars that would likely not be included in Mr. Gardiner's missive to Mr. Bennet. Elizabeth was unsure how they would pass the days until her father and sister arrived. She was certain only they would travel north for the nuptials. Though Mrs. Bennet would be cross, she could not attend the first wedding of one of her daughters. And that brought her mind back to the situation of Wickham. How would they manage this without him escaping or their reputations getting ruined?

"With just the two of them traveling north," explained her uncle, "it would be quite easy to present the trip as a father accompanying his married daughter as she ventured to join her husband. That will lend credence to the story that Lydia and Wickham were already wed. And with us touring Derbyshire, it would make sense that Mr. Bennet would join us and then travel back to Hertfordshire." He nodded twice. "Yes, that story will suffice."

"But how will we keep Wickham hidden and quiet? And how are we all to share one room?" Elizabeth inquired.

And there was a more concerning matter that she did not mention, how were they to keep silent on the subject around Mr. Darcy's sister? Elizabeth felt uneasy keeping such a secret from the young, innocent girl. The same girl Wickham had tried to seduce and elope with years earlier.

"Wickham cannot stay here at the inn," stated Mr. Gardiner, who scowled. "That is something I need to discuss with Mr. Darcy."

Elizabeth frowned at the words she had just penned, glistening as they dried, catching her eye as she thought about what her uncle had said. It was another reason why it was unsettling Mr. Darcy had departed quickly. Was her betrothed not even going to provide assistance in the matter? But he had tracked down Wickham's location, which showed he was not averse to helping. She tossed her head. She could not make heads or tails of the man's behavior.

A maid knocked on the door and handed a note to Mr. Gardiner. "For you, sir." She proffered the stationary. "The servants are in the hall awaiting your instructions."

Elizabeth and Mrs. Gardiner shared confused glances. Mr. Gardiner raised his head from reading the note and smiled. "That is the problem solved, then. Mr. Darcy has sent servants to accompany Wickham to his mother's house, where he will be guarded until the wedding."

That was an easy solution, and relief settled upon her. But, she still was uneasy. Mr. Darcy could have brought the news himself. Dread grew in her chest. But there was nothing to be done for it now. She had to marry him to save her and her family's reputation. And it was too late for her heart as well. She had already lost it to him.

But no matter what that man thought, she would treat their upcoming marriage with the same regard as if she was marrying the man of her dreams. Which had been Mr. Darcy for quite some time.

The trio quit their private sitting room and watched Wickham as he was helped down the staircase to the waiting carriage. The poor man had suddenly taken ill, was the story they shared with any onlookers. Though Elizabeth was sure that several had deciphered that there had to be another reason, as there were far too many servants.

THE NEXT DAY WAS SUNDAY, and they departed the inn to walk the short distance to the little church in Lambton. Elizabeth had not anticipated Mr. Darcy to wait for her by the front doors. However, some signs that he still planned to marry her or even had some affection would not go amiss.

They entered the church, nodding at some of the people and old friends of Mrs. Gardiner they had met. She noticed Mr. Darcy and Georgiana's heads in the first row. Elizabeth glanced away and followed her uncle and aunt into a pew. Her fingers dug into her hymnal as she sighed. It would be a long service.

She fidgeted, someone coughed, then Elizabeth looked up again and stilled. Mr. Darcy was in profile. It looked like he was searching for someone, her. Hope leaped in her chest, but the pastor walked to the lectern, and Mr. Darcy faced forward again.

The service seemed to last an interminably long time, though she was sure only the usual time had elapsed. After the service, as the wooden pews creaked while congregants prepared for the service to be finished, the pastor announced he had Banns to read. Elizabeth's heart skipped. But the Banns were read for the upcoming nuptials of Lawrence Ahearn and Nora Malvey.

Elizabeth bowed her head, hope dying in her chest, as the hard edge of her hymnal dug into her fingers. The pastor then announced the Banns for Mr. Darcy and Elizabeth Bennet. She felt a blush creep over her cheeks as Mrs. Gardiner squeezed her hand. She could not restrain her smile, even as loud whispers filled the air.

The congregation exited the church by pew, the front pews departing first. Elizabeth composed herself before their pew's turn to leave and face the scrutiny of the locals. Mr. Darcy shared a glance and a small smile with her as he walked by with Georgiana, followed by Mr. Bingley, Miss Bingley, and the Hursts.

She had just exited when her uncle shifted, and she saw Mr. Darcy standing to the side, almost surrounded by well-wishers. His friends were standing near him, but Miss Bingley was closest to him. Elizabeth stepped closer and then stilled at what she had heard.

"Much felicitations to you and your betrothed, Mr. Darcy. She must be something special for you to offer and finally settle down." An old woman stood before him, now looking at Miss Bingley. "I am so pleased Pemberley will have a mistress again, and you will do such a fine job, Miss Bennet, I can tell."

Elizabeth had a perfect view, in between the crowd surrounding Mr. Darcy, to see the woman's words' effect on Miss Bingley. Quickly she covered her mouth before laughter could escape.

"Pardon me, this is not my betrothed but my friend's sister, Miss Bingley. My betrothed," Mr. Darcy desperately scanned the crowd, "is exiting the church yet or is lost in the crush here. May I introduce Miss Bingley?"

A hand squeezed her arm, and Mrs. Gardiner's whispered voice laced with amusement reached her ears. "Oh, dear. You had better go and stand by your man."

As Elizabeth pushed through the well-wishers, relief and pride shone on Mr. Darcy's face. "Here she is." He raised an arm and clasped her arm in his as she reached his side. "May I present my betrothed, Miss Elizabeth Bennet from Hertfordshire. "

Elizabeth greeted the townspeople and accepted their good wishes until all that remained were the Gardiners, the Darcys, and Mr. Bingley. He answered a questioning look from Mr. Darcy while running his fingers through his hair. "Er, my sister Caroline felt unwell and returned to Pemberley with the Hursts."

She bit the inside of her cheek and lowered her head to stifle the smile threatening to show.

"I would invite you to Pemberley for luncheon, but I must leave. I am departing to London for business."

Raising her head, she was caught by Mr. Darcy's intense stare. She blinked and glanced at Georgiana, standing next to her brother.

"But I am certain my sister will be issuing you many an invitation during my absence." Georgiana shyly smiled but still looked as if hosting guests was tantamount to inviting spiders into one's bedroom.

Mr. Darcy grabbed Elizabeth's hand and squeezed. Then with valedictions and regrets that sudden business was taking him away from her, he departed for his carriage with Mr. Bingley and Georgiana.

CHAPTER 14

*E*lizabeth and the Gardiners did not broach the subject of the sudden business needs of Mr. Darcy until they were in their private rooms after devouring a satisfying meal of shepherd's pie. Their conversation was quickly curtailed by a note delivered to Elizabeth. She recognized the penmanship. It was a note from Mr. Darcy about why he was traveling to London. He was accompanying Wickham to procure a special license.

She was gratified for a reason, as the worry that Lydia's actual matrimonial state would be uncovered, and stain their family, had not abated. Elizabeth would only be at ease once Wickham and her sister were wed. But that did not mean that she did not wish Mr. Darcy had not needed to travel and be gone for several days. However, she would remain close to him as she expected invitations from Georgiana to dine at Pemberley. And with her spirits high again now that she was no longer concerned regarding his affection towards her, Elizabeth had a good night's sleep. The first since the news of Lydia's perfidy had reached them.

The next day Elizabeth rose and dressed carefully, for she was expecting an invitation from Georgiana. She was looking forward to spending time with her soon-to-be sister-in-law and Mr. Bingley, but not so much the man's sisters. Without Mr. Darcy present, she was sure their ill natures would reassert themselves.

But her plans for the day took an unexpected turn when a maid burst into their private sitting room to announce visitors. The Gardiners and Elizabeth exchanged astonished glances. Why would Georgiana call on them? But it was not the expected younger Darcy who entered the room, but Mr. and Mrs. Bennet. Followed by the entire rest of the Bennet family.

Elizabeth gaped as her mother recounted their travel misfortunes to the room.

"It was the most horrific thing, to be sure," said Mrs. Bennet, wearily collapsing onto the settee. "To travel all night hours and be so cramped in that carriage. I am sure I shall never get over it."

Mr. Bennet slowly nodded as he claimed the armchair by the fireplace. "It was quite an ordeal. We had to stop every few hours to change horses."

Lydia, who usually had no lack of spirits, slouched next to her mother. "I do not know why we could not get into our rooms. This is an inn. Do they not have rooms ready for travelers coming by?"

"Indeed, my thoughts exactly, Lydia!" Mrs. Bennet lifted a hand before dropping it to the cushions.

Servants brought another table and chairs into the already crowded room. Kitty and Mary sank down at the next table. Elizabeth glanced away and analyzed Jane's face as she sat down next to her at the table, exhibiting the strain of the arduous travel.

"I do not understand why we had to travel overnight," Lydia complained. "We could not even stay at an inn and rest. We had to sleep sitting up in the carriage!"

Elizabeth closed her eyes. She had missed her family, but some of them not so much. Thankfully, Mr. Gardiner responded as to why their timely arrival was essential, which enabled Elizabeth to lean near Jane. "How can this be? Papa was to arrive with only Lydia. It will not be possible to keep her silent here. Nor Mama!"

"Mama would not miss the first wedding of one of her daughters. She could not be deterred, and Lydia did not want her family to miss her wedding. Especially with all her friends, the officer's wives, still in Brighton."

Elizabeth leaned back in her chair and closed her eyes. Impulsive Lydia. But the blame did not fall solely on her shoulders. She glanced at her parent's table, where Mrs. Bennet was leaning towards their table.

"—the best fashion houses in London! Can you imagine not being allowed to order a new trousseau? My dearest Lydia had to travel north to be wed in clothes she already had! Have you ever heard such a thing?"

Elizabeth sighed. Her plans for the day and foreseeable future were going to include something other than

Pemberley. The reason why her family had arrived and who Lydia was to marry had to be kept secret from Georgiana. And the townsfolk. Therefore Lydia and Mrs. Bennet, who could not comprehend the severity, had to be kept away from anyone outside the family. Or the entire family's reputation would be destroyed.

And she was sure that if this knowledge got out, Mr. Darcy would have to withdraw his suit. Though there was great disapproval and censure of a man that broke an engagement, there were reasons when it was tolerable. A sister of his future bride running away with a man, with no wedding taking place, was one of those reasons. Elizabeth rubbed the sides of her forehead.

"Why can I not be with my beloved Wickham? We are in the same town, and I have not seen him for a fortnight." The Gardiners hushed Lydia. Mr. Bennet even looked up from his plate and told his youngest daughter to behave or she would be sent to their room.

Dread settled in Elizabeth's chest. Keeping this secret from Pemberley and the entire town seemed impossible. If only Mr. Darcy could acquire that special license and return quickly, the sooner Lydia and Wickham were married.

ELIZABETH FLUNG open the door to her room, stepping aside so that Jane could enter before shutting the door. "It is a modest chamber, but it is immaculate. The maid is meticulous, and the owners are incredibly hospitable. It shall be like we are back home at Longbourn, sharing a room."

Jane unpacked her valise onto the bed and then clasped her hands with her sister's. "How have you been, Lizzy? Your letters were so—"

"What you mean is that they hardly revealed anything at all."

She gave Elizabeth's hands an affectionate squeeze. "Yes, Lizzy. I cannot imagine how you must have felt engaged to be married to Mr. Darcy? I know how much you detest him. And I cannot fathom what Mr. Gardiner meant in his letter: it was through no fault of yours or Mr. Darcy. And then your letter, Lizzy," she reproached her laughing sister. "You stated livestock were at fault."

Elizabeth shook her head, chuckling while she sat down on the bed. After a long sigh, she looked at the smoke-stained ceiling before lowering her gaze to her rapt sister. "Oh Jane, I scarcely know where to begin. I am not even sure you shall believe what I tell you. It is so unbelievable."

"How did you become compromised?"

She chuckled softly, then related a shortened version of events that occurred that fateful day they toured Pemberley. Jane gasped and made sounds at all the right moments. "Oh, Lizzy! I cannot believe it!" She slowly shook her head. "Only to you would something like this occur."

"It is better that it happened to me and not anyone else. I find absurdity amusing."

Jane leaned over to hold her sister's hand, anxiety back on her features. "Lizzy, I know your nature is such to make the best of every situation, but you can be honest with me. I know you always desired to marry for nothing but love."

Elizabeth looked at her, smiling, so relieved that her sister grinned in return. "Oh Jane, I adore him deeply. He is the most agreeable of men."

"Lizzy! Mr. Darcy?"

Elizabeth laughed while nodding. "I requested him to court me. He has changed, oh Jane, he is the perfect gentleman. No man could measure up to him."

"I am thankful for you, then."

It was a heartrending smile on her sister's face. She knew Jane was still pained over Mr. Bingley and treasured him still. Elizabeth held her sister's hand tight and prayed that situation would pleasingly solve itself now that they were both back in the same county again. And would, without fail, see each other again at Pemberley.

THE DAYS PASSED SLOWLY with Lydia and Mrs. Bennet's endless complaining and whinging about how unfair it was to be cooped inside. Mrs. Bennet would enter Elizabeth's room, where she had been conversing with her aunt and Jane, followed by Lydia and Kitty. During those occasions, Elizabeth would have much embroidery work to unravel and fix.

"I cannot comprehend why we have not been invited to Pemberley, this palatial home everyone talked of in Hertfordshire? You are his betrothed, and he has not called on you or extended an invitation! Poor etiquette. I expected more from someone with—"

"Mama! Mr. Darcy is away on business, and we must keep our family's reputation secure."

Mrs. Bennet pouted. "It is unjust your beau gets to roam about society when Lydia and her intended are compelled to remain inside. It is unhealthy for the mind to be enclosed all the time!"

"Mrs. Bennet, please."

Not even Mrs. Gardiner's entreaty stilled Mrs. Bennet's statements. Elizabeth set down the pillow-case she had been stitching, for she would have to cut and sew where she had pulled the red thread through the yellow flowers. Standing, she walked to the small writing desk and removed a sheet of stationery to answer Georgiana's latest letter.

Elizabeth had written the girl that she had come down with an illness, and their exchanging letters had commenced. She wished heartily that she could abandon the inn and was even willing to endure the presence of the Bingley sisters. Still, any invitation would include the Gardiners, leaving only Mr. Bennet to restrain Lydia and Mrs. Bennet.

Her letter writing to Georgiana was disrupted by the sudden pounding at the door. Elizabeth jolted, scattering ink across the letter. She sighed. The letter would have to be thrown out and a new sheet used.

"Who can that be? Your sisters would not knock." Mrs. Gardiner peered between the two elder Bennet sisters.

"Perhaps it is Papa?" Jane made to set aside her embroidery and stand.

Elizabeth held out a hand. "Let me answer the door. I am closest and not as invested in my embroidery as you are."

With her face flushed and eyes wide, a maid bobbed a curtsy. "Ma'am, you have a visitor, Lady Catherine de Bourgh."

Elizabeth stood speechless, then brushed the front of her day dress to remove any leftover shavings from when she had repaired her quill.

Mrs. Gardiner advanced. "Is this the woman whose estate you visited last year?"

"Yes, Rosings Park, my friend Charlotte married Mr. Collins, the parson."

"I hope she has not come bearing bad news."

Elizabeth doubted the great Lady Catherine would have traveled such a distance to inform her of bad news regarding Charlotte. Then she frowned and pondered how the woman knew of her residing in Lambton at that inn. Foreboding settled in her stomach as she followed the maid down the stairs to the private sitting room where the lady stood waiting for her. The woman was still in her traveling cloak and had not removed her hat.

"Madam, to what do I owe the honor of such a visit?"

Lady Catherine's lips pursed. "You can be at no loss to discern the reason for my journey, Miss Bennet."

"Indeed, you are mistaken. I am quite unable to explain the honor of seeing you here."

"Miss Bennet, you ought to recognize I am not to be trifled with. But however insincere you choose to be, you shall not find me so. A report of an alarming nature reached me. I was told not only had your sister made an advantageous match but that you, Miss Bennet, would soon be united with my nephew, Mr. Darcy."

Elizabeth stared, clasping her hands in front.

"Though I know it must be a scandalous falsehood, I instantly resolved to make my sentiments known. Only I discovered that you were in Derbyshire, and the Banns have been read!"

Lady Catherine circled Elizabeth, who glanced away. "Your arts and allurements may have caused him to forget what he owes to himself and his family. You may have ensnared him, but you will end this now."

"If the Banns have been read, I am at a loss as to what you expect me to do?"

Lady Catherine closed her eyes. "Do you know who I am?"

Elizabeth stiffly stared at the woman.

"My nephew has been destined for my daughter, a union desired by both their mothers. I will not be obstructed by the upstart pretensions of a young woman without family ties or fortune! This connection can never take place. Now, what do you say?"

"If it is his wish to marry me, then what you say or do will not impede him. You are wasting your time, as well as mine. I am sure you must be fatigued from your travels."

Lady Catherine slammed her cane on the floor. "I am not accustomed to comportment such as this! Is this to be endured? It shall not be. Your alliance will be a disgrace. Your name would never be mentioned by any of us."

"These would be grievous misfortunes, indeed."

"Obstinate, headstrong girl! I am ashamed of you. You will call off this farce immediately. I am not in the habit of brooking disappointment."

"That will make your ladyship's position at present more miserable, but that will have no impact on me."

The older woman's eyes narrowed. "If you were sensible of your own good, you would not wish to quit the sphere in which you have been brought up."

Elizabeth turned away, walking to the door. "I implore you to not importune me any further on the subject."

"Not so swift, I have another objection. Your youngest sister's infamous elopement. I know it all. Is such a girl to be my nephew's sister-in-law? Are the shades of—"

Elizabeth opened the door and strode out of the sitting room and down the hall. Lady Catherine's voice followed her.

"—Pemberley to be thus polluted? Unfeeling, selfish girl! You decline to oblige me to pay respect, honor, and gratitude! Very well, I shall know how to act."

CHAPTER 15

*M*r. Darcy sighed in relief as the familiar countryside of Derbyshire sprawled out the carriage window. He had not enjoyed the trip for several reasons, the uppermost of which was his traveling companion, Mr. Wickham. The man had no morals, scruples, regret, or contrition over his actions. The scoundrel had attempted to slip away at each posting change. Mr. Darcy was quite glad he had brought extra servants with him to guard Wickham. When they reached London, Mr. Darcy was under no illusion that if they had stayed the night in his townhouse in Mayfair, by morning, Wickham would be gone.

This was why, after securing the special license from the bishop, he did not inform Wickham of his plans.

Not even when the wretch had commented that it would be delightful to see the Darcy townhouse again. Only when they were heading out of London did Wickham realize they were immediately heading back to Derbyshire and Lambton.

Wickham was sullen the entire trip back. But with two strapping stable lads in the carriage with them, the louse had no opportunity to escape or cause a diversion to cover his flight. No, Mr. Darcy would not let that man out of his or his servant's sights until the wedding to Lydia Bennet had occurred. Then he would thankfully see the man gone.

The carriage pulled to a stop in front of Mrs. Wickham's small home, and the two strapping stable lads joined the waiting servants stationed outside the house. As Wickham sullenly descended the carriage steps, Mr. Darcy reminded him, "Your wedding will be on the morrow at 8 A.M."

He rapped on the carriage ceiling, then was jerked back against the bench as the carriage rolled off toward Pemberley. All the extra servants pulling double-duty guarding Wickham deserved extra pay this week. He would immediately order his steward to take care of the matter upon his return to

Pemberley. After a hot bath and a hot meal. But first, he would let his sister know he was home.

Mr. Darcy sighed and leaned his head back. Rarely did he push so hard, but he knew time was of the essence in this matter. He could not wait for the comforts of home and loathed being on the road but detested it even more when traveling into the night. It was not safe, but with many outriders, all armed, they had not experienced any trouble.

The carriage made the final turn onto the drive to Pemberley, and he could scarcely stay seated. Before the servants could pull out the steps, he leaped out of the carriage and bounded up the front steps. His Hessian boots clacked on the marble floor of the foyer.

"Please inform my sister that I am home and have a bath and meal brought to my room." Mr. Darcy paused and eyed the footman, who shared wide-eyed glances with the footman standing on the other side of the front doors. "Is something—"

"Is that my nephew?"

Mr. Darcy froze, then slowly turned in horror towards the sound of a cane thumping along the sitting room floor.

A footman behind his shoulder whispered, "She arrived two days ago, sir."

Georgiana burst out of the sitting room, nearly sprinting to engulf him in a hug. Never had his sister greeted him after a trip in such a manner. Things must have been challenging indeed with his aunt present.

Lady Catherine de Bourgh's shrill voice preceded her entrance. "Georgiana Darcy, it is not lady-like to run!"

Mr. Darcy tightened his arms around his sister's shoulders. "What has happened? You are shaking. Are you unwell?"

Georgiana's fingers tightened on the back of his jacket. "She arrived two days ago and has been in high dudgeon. The things she has said about Miss Bennet!"

He pulled back from his sister with Lady Catherine's approach. Georgiana slipped out from under his arm and stood partially behind him.

"Where have you been? I had not planned to find you away from home upon my arrival. What business would you have in London that was so urgent?"

Mr. Darcy stiffened, fighting back his impulsive response. "I had not received notice of your impending arrival, Aunt."

"Yes, yes, I am most displeased, though." She squinted at him, but it failed to affect him in any way except to inflame his ire. "You are engaged to my daughter and have been since the cradle, yet you had Banns read for—"

"Madam." He felt Georgiana slide further behind him. "I must demand that you refrain from this line of inquiry. My personal business is my own."

Movement on the steps drew his attention. Mr. Bingley had halted in his descent of the main staircase. Mr. Darcy was relieved to observe a friendly face. However, he would not have begrudged the man for quitting the place when his curmudgeonly relative had arrived. "Bingley, I hope you found ways to entertain yourself while I was absent?"

His friend's face brightened, and he quickly descended the staircase. "There is no end to the amusements that can be had at—"

"I will not be interrupted!"

His smile fell while Mr. Bingley stopped his progress on the staircase. Mr. Darcy slowly turned and narrowed his gaze upon his aunt, standing alone. Georgiana, he realized, was currently hiding behind his back. He would have much to make up for leaving his sister alone with their aunt in his absence. Yet, he could not have expected her arrival during his absence nor her abominable rudeness.

"I will not have you speak of my betrothed in such a manner, especially in my own home."

Lady Catherine de Bourgh stepped closer. "You cannot possibly plan to continue this charade. Your duty to your family, honor, and obligation requires that you—"

"Aunt, I have tolerated your behavior due to our association, but I will not tolerate it anymore. Cease this immediately, or I will ask you to leave."

"You cannot oust me. I am nobility! And your aunt, —"

Mr. Darcy stepped towards her, his hands clenched. "I will do what I must. One more word against *my betrothed* or her family, and I will have your bags packed and loaded on your carriage."

His aunt clenched her jaw and glared. Mr. Darcy
turned and strode up the steps passing a speechless
Mr. Bingley, and stormed down the hallway to his
rooms. He tore off his cravat, closed his bedroom
door, and nearly ripped his buttons, removing his
waistcoat. Thankfully his valet arrived to help him
complete his undressing.

The ordinarily verbose man was silent, which did
not help to improve Mr. Darcy's mood. He had
always taken great pains to behave as the perfect
gentleman, in which not raising his voice was nearly
at the top of the list of requirements. And yet his
display in the foyer had even shocked his friend. Mr.
Darcy groaned and rubbed his face, the hot water
from the bath soothing his tired eyes and aching
head.

He stood from the bath, wishing he could have
soaked until the water grew cold, but he had guests
that had been left to the not-so-tender mercies of his
aunt and a sister that had been discountenanced by
the same said aunt.

After dressing and consuming a hastily supped light
repast, he found Georgiana in her room. "I must
apologize, sister. I made the trip as rapidly as possi-

ble, yet I would have ridden through the night had I known that our aunt had arrived in my absence."

Georgiana stood from where she had been sitting on her bed looking at fashion plates and hurried over to envelop him in another embrace. "It is not your fault." In a whisper, she continued, "It is Lady Catherine's."

Mr. Darcy smiled for the first time that day as he wrapped his arms around her shoulders and kissed her head. "I hope she was not too much to bear, but that would be inconceivable. Tell me, are the Bingley sisters still in residence? I saw only their brother."

She sighed long enough for him to know that things had not gone well in more than one quarter. "Miss Bingley and Lady Catherine shared many of the same sentiments about Miss Bennet. I do not know why because she has been most amiable. They said most unkind things."

Mr. Darcy was not surprised at his aunt's behavior, but he could not say the same for Miss Bingley's. She had voiced her dislike of the Bennets and Elizabeth in particular quite plainly on several occasions. But for her to admonish his intended in his own house was too much. He would speak to Bingley, though he knew his friend would not relish restraining his sister; it had to be done. He hoped he could convey the seriousness of his request to Bingley. Because he would not hesitate to have Miss Bingley removed from Pemberley if she did not cease in her haranguing of Miss Bennet.

Georgiana pulled back from their embrace with a mischievous smile. "Do you know that Miss Bennet and I have been exchanging letters? We are so close that a servant can ride back and forth between Lambton and Pemberley several times in one day!"

Her giggles turned into laughter at the expression on her brother's face.

"May I inquire as to the nature of your correspondence?" He could not envision any subject two new acquaintances could discuss that would result in his sister's amusement.

"I wrote her first to cheer her spirits as she had sent a note that she was unwell and could not accept any invitations."

He frowned that she would not want to visit her future home. Had she been unwell, or was this a contrived reason to stay away from Pemberley? Or had she thought to stay away for fear of disclosing

Mr. Darcy's rationale for his abrupt business in London? But then, dread settled as he cast upon one reason that seemed more likely than all others. "Did Miss Bennet happen to give another reason?"

Georgiana tilted her head. "Do you think she was not unwell?"

Blast it all. What had he done? "Not at all. Miss Bennet is honest and kind. If she was unwell, then she was truly so. No, I wondered...if somehow she heard that Lady Catherine was in residence and had chosen to stay away though I am sure she would… have adored…."

He trailed off at Georgiana's slap of hands over her mouth and then at her bursting laughter.

"Miss Bennet knew Lady Catherine was here because I told her! She had the best ideas for hiding and avoiding Aunt and Miss Bingley." She lowered her hands, beaming. "I cannot wait for her to be my sister!"

Mr. Darcy smiled again, his heart warming even more towards the woman he had missed the most.

CHAPTER 16

$\mathcal{M}$r. Darcy strode down the hallway in the east wing to the main staircase. He had not divulged his plans for this morning to his excellent friend Bingley, knowing the man could not keep a secret. And this was one secret that he most assuredly did not want to get to Georgiana and his aunt. His sister would be unable to keep the secret quiet, and his aunt would stop at nothing to stop the wedding.

He bounded down the steps to the carriage waiting below in the dark morning light. He had departed earlier than necessary to escort Wickham to the church, expecting a desperate man's last attempts for freedom. Mr. Darcy leaned back against the swaying carriage, determined not to fall asleep.

When the conveyance rolled to a stop in front of Mrs. Wickham's house, Mr. Darcy was not surprised to find the scoundrel's mother wiping her eyes. She had admirably raised him despite his father being a drunkard and her son a wretch.

"Georgie, I do not understand why you cannot take a commission with a closer regiment? Why you will be stationed near to the wilds of Scotland!"

Mr. Wickham smiled amiably as he escorted his mother out of her home. "Mama," he glanced at Mr. Darcy with a conspiratorial look, "you know how the militia is. I must go where I am needed."

"You are such a good lad, so dedicated to the Crown and the good of country. I just wish they did not need you so far north."

Mr. Darcy arched his eyebrow but did not refute the apparent lie Wickham had fed his mother. He would let the woman enjoy seeing her son married on this day. In just a few hours, he would be rid of the wretch. Hopefully, their paths would never cross again.

He stood aside as Wickham handed his mother into the carriage. Then waited until Wickham stopped motioning for Darcy to enter and finally climbed in, taking a seat next to his elderly mother. The ride to the church was mercifully short. Sitting across from the smug man basking under his mother's compliments was nearly too much to bear.

But he had known the man since they were young lads and saw Wickham's fiddling with his jacket and cravat as signs that the scoundrel recognized this was his final chance for freedom.

Mr. Darcy disembarked at the church, standing alone in the gravel driveway, waiting for Mrs. Wickham to alight with her arthritic knees. He checked his pocket watch and noted the time. He was correct in his assumption that Wickham would delay matters. They only had a few minutes before the wedding was scheduled to begin. And the local parson was a stickler for punctuality.

But Wickham once descended from the well-sprung and appointed carriage, stood in the drive straightening his jacket. Mr. Darcy gestured to the front of the church.

"You would begrudge me my last moments of freedom?" the man guilefully queried.

"This moment is of your making." Mr. Darcy gestured again to the church. "Wickham, your bride is waiting inside."

Wickham, sensing no quarter, sheepishly smiled, then raised his chin and strode to the front doors of the small, white church, his mother clinging to his arm and crying. An outrider that had accompanied the carriage opened the door, leaving nothing to chance, for this was a prime opportunity for a last mad dash to freedom. Mr. Darcy had gone so far as to position several men around the church itself. No matter where the man ran, he would be dragged back into this church to marry the youngest Bennet girl that had fallen prey to the scoundrel.

But no desperate ploys were attempted, and Mr. Darcy breathed a sigh of relief as he followed them into the church. The gloom of the interior covered him with the closing bang of the door. Once his eyes adjusted, he was already so far up the aisle that he only saw Elizabeth's profile. Mrs. Bennet's sobbing and not-so-quiet pleas for Lydia to write often and travel to Hertfordshire as soon as she could followed them up the aisle. Then he had to turn away to enter the pew to fulfill his duty as a witness and best man.

Mrs. Wickham trailed him in the pew patting his arm after she sat. "I am so glad you are here, Fitzwilliam. You were such close pals as boys."

He grunted and continued to stare at the empty altar, trying to ignore the continued chatter of Lydia and the passionate pleas from her eldest sisters for her to quiet down. Mr. Darcy yearned to sit next to Elizabeth, hold her hand and look into her eyes. A quick glance around Wickham showed the profile of her blue bonnet sticking out past her sister's hats.

The parson entered, crossing the altar, causing Darcy to regretfully tear his gaze away and stand facing the front. Mrs. Bennet's sobs grew louder as the wedding service commenced, with both bride and groom exiting their pews to stand in front of the solemn parson.

Lydia clung to Wickham's arm and stared up unabashedly at her soon-to-be husband before the parson coughed and bade her face him. Mr. Darcy looked askance at the only reason he was involved in this travesty, his heart leaping as Elizabeth's brown eyes met his and softened.

The service concluded quickly, with the Wickhams cheerfully traipsing down the aisle with Lydia glowing. She hung onto her new husband with both arms as Mrs. Bennet fretted and cried at losing her youngest and favorite child so far to the north. The Gardiners and Bennets stood back from the happy couple. Kitty stood between them and the rest, perhaps uncertain whether to be happy for her sister as the mood of the others was disapproval.

"Haven't I snared myself a handsome husband?"

Mrs. Bennet dabbed her eyes. "Indeed, you have, my love."

Mr. Wickham beamed. Mr. Darcy averted his gaze, catching Elizabeth's face, which matched his own.

"You are very kind, sir."

"You are all goodness and benevolence, ma'am, as always." Wickham bowed.

Mr. Darcy rolled his eyes.

"Oh, let me give you a kiss, then." Mrs. Bennet kissed her new son-in-law's cheek as Lydia smirked at her sisters.

"What a pity we didn't all go to Brighton. I could have obtained husbands for all my sisters!"

"Lydia!"

Mr. Darcy looked away, noticing that Jane was more subdued than the rest, staring down at the gravel drive. Scrutiny of her features revealed sadness, which prompted a twinge of regret in his chest. He could only assume the girl was reminiscing about the love she had lost thanks to his intervention. He would have to remedy that, especially now that both were in the same county, with one even residing at Pemberley.

"Oh, do you have to leave so soon? Why can't we have a wedding breakfast for them?" Mrs. Bennet wailed. "And Mr. Bennet so cruel as to refuse to take us into the North Country."

Mary spoke up. "I should refuse to go, in any case."

"Oh, keep your mouth shut, girl! Who asked you?" Mrs. Bennet turned back to the newly married couple. "Oh, Lydia, you will write to me frequently, won't you?" Mrs. Bennet embraced her daughter, still clinging to Wickham.

"Well, I don't know. We married women don't have much time for writing. My sisters may write to me. They will have nothing better to do, as I shall."

Mr. Darcy looked away.

The Wickhams clambered into their hired hack, Lydia leaning out the window waving her small bouquet at the gathering. Only Kitty and Mrs. Bennet waved as they were finally taken away.

He spun round at the sound of someone approaching. When he saw it was Elizabeth, his formerly severe expression softened.

"Please permit me…to thank you on behalf of all my family since…they don't know to whom they are obligated."

"If you will thank me, let it be for yourself alone. Your family owes me nothing. As much as I esteem them, I think I thought solely of you."

Her smile and fondness directed his way, brought a smile to his lips and an ardent wish that they were somewhere else, alone.

"I understand you and my sister kept in contact. "

Elizabeth giggled. "Oh yes, your sister is delightful! We had great mirth exchanging letters." Then her expression became serious. "I hope you don't begrudge my subterfuge with your sister, telling her I was sick. I couldn't have her calling on me at the inn with my sister Lydia in residence."

He reached out to her but dropped his hand after a glance showed they had her relative's undivided attention. "You acted as any lady would." He cleared his throat. "Lady Catherine informed me of her meeting with you. I may say that her revelation had quite the contrary effect to what she meant."

Elizabeth's eyes laughed as she smiled.

"I knew that had you truly decided against me, you would have admitted it openly."

"Yes, you know enough of my frankness to believe me capable of that!"

They stared at each other with tenderness until the enchantment was broken by the approach of Mr. Bennet. "Well, we had better depart for the inn. Kitty, I fear, will expire of hunger shortly."

Mr. Darcy glanced away, his eyes resting on the solemn eldest Bennet daughter. "Mr. Bennet and family, Mr. and Mrs. Gardiner, I would like to invite you to Pemberley to dine for supper this evening. I am afraid my chef would resign if I asked you for lunch."

Elizabeth's eyes glowed as her relatives filled the air with gratitude and enthusiasm. "Thank you, but isn't your aunt still in residence?"

He nodded. "I surmise an audience may curtail my aunt's presumptuous behavior. Plus," he glanced at Jane, "there is someone your sister has an acquaintance with presently staying at Pemberley."

His pleasure was immediate with the happy smile on his betrothed's face. He reached out and held her hand, wishing again that they did not have an audience.

"Oh, Lizzy, with you married next, I will have two daughters wedded. I shall be so lonesome with my daughters leaving me!"

Mr. Darcy bowed and excused himself, boarding his carriage. He would accommodate Elizabeth's mother for her sake. But, he would not extend his time exposed to her silliness if possible. Besides, he had to warn Cook to anticipate eight more for supper.

CHAPTER 17

 r. Darcy leaped out of the carriage and waited for his sister as she descended slowly behind him. He adjusted his jacket, then took Georgiana's arm in his and ascended the front staircase of Pemberley. He had missed Elizabeth during his several day's journey with Wickham. He could not wait till later that day when she would be back under his roof. He imagined her eyes glittering in the candlelight of the supper, her angelic voice crooning while playing the pianoforte he had gifted Georgiana just a few weeks ago.

"Brother, I cannot run up the stairs. I will trip and fall."

He paused, realizing that he had almost been sprinting up the staircase, so intent was he on his musings. "I apologize. I was lost in thought."

Georgiana turned to him. "I have not seen you this animated since you arranged that picnic for Elizabeth. The one with the sheep that was loose!" She giggled.

Mr. Darcy felt a momentary embarrassment at being so easily readable by his younger sister. But then he realized he did not mind. She knew how joyous and elated he was to see Elizabeth again at Pemberley. "I have yearned for her company."

Georgiana halted on the terrace. He spun to her with a raised eyebrow. "Will our aunt—I am—" she sighed and gazed down at their locked hands. "I am scared of what Lady Catherine will say to Miss Bennet."

Mr. Darcy compressed his lips and scowled at the front doors. "Do not worry. I shall have a talk with our aunt."

After entering their home, Mr. Darcy asked for the housekeeper to be summoned. Ever efficient, Mrs. Reynolds had anticipated him and was waiting near his study.

"Inform Cook we shall be expecting eight more for supper tonight. Any costs for the meal will be permitted. Miss Bennet and her family, including the Gardiners, will join us."

Mrs. Reynolds opened her mouth, most likely to ask a question, but it was not her voice he heard.

"Is that my nephew? Did I hear you say there are visitors for supper?"

Lady Catherine de Bourgh marched out of the sitting room, her cane striking against the foyer's marble floor with every step. "Are you carrying through with this? I have told you—"

Mr. Darcy faced the older woman, his patience worn thin. "Miss Bennet is my fiancée, and I will be marrying her. I have invited her family—"

"You are persisting with this farce?" Her expression was one of disgust. "She has no connections, no fortune. Her youngest sister recently—"

"I would ask you to cease that sentence, madam."

"This shall not be accepted!" She punctuated the statement with a thud of her cane reverberating throughout the foyer.

He felt his sister cower behind his back. Mr. Darcy wondered again what it had been like for his sister with their aunt in residence while he was gone.

"You have been promised to my daughter a match agreed upon by both mothers—"

Mr. Darcy pivoted to Mrs. Reynolds, cutting his aunt off. "Please ensure my aunt's bags are packed and her carriage readied. She will be leaving Pemberley immediately."

His aunt's cry reverberated through the hall. "You cannot expel me. I am your mother's only sister!"

He escorted his sister up the main staircase, passed the wide eyes of the Bingleys on the second floor, and down the hall to the family bedrooms. Their aunt continued her tirade about the perils of country girls influencing men with their wiles and temptations until the slam of his bedroom door silenced her voice.

MR. DARCY DESCENDED the front steps to wait for carriages to finish traveling down the drive to the house. He swept a hand down the front of his jacket as Mr. Bingley's footsteps sounded behind him. His friend had escorted Georgiana, as Mr. Darcy wished to ensure he was present for the arrival of his intended.

"The entire Bennet family, you say?"

He nodded but kept his eyes fixed on the first carriage rolling past the final turn to the house. He had just completed an unpleasant but necessary task in his study: informing his good friend of the concealment he and Mr. Bingley's sisters had undertaken when Jane Bennet had been in London for several months. Mr. Darcy apologized for his part in the scheme to separate the two.

Mr. Bingley had such a genial nature that his anger blew over quickly. Now, he was standing next to Mr. Darcy, fidgeting, anticipating seeing Jane again with the knowledge that she cared for him. And it was evident that his friend had never stopped caring for the eldest Bennet daughter. Mr. Darcy sighed, relieved that, finally, he could mend his abhorrent mistake.

Mr. Darcy tugged at the sleeves on his jacket again and then clasped his hands behind his back to suppress his fidgeting. There was no valid reason for his nervousness except that he wanted this reunion between Jane and Bingley to transpire without a hitch. His intention was primarily for Elizabeth to recognize that he had done this for her. If Elizabeth's sister felt anything like Bingley, he was confident they would be engaged within a sennight. Perhaps even four days.

The two carriages rolled to a stop, Mr. Bingley's eyes darting from one to the other uncertain of which held the woman he yearned to see. Mr. Darcy and his friend were disheartened when the first carriage divulged the Bennet family, minus the two eldest daughters. They were in the second carriage, descending the steps after the Gardiners.

Mr. Darcy ceased studying Bingley and Jane's reunion when a gasp caught his attention. Elizabeth's eyes lit up at seeing her sister and his friend reuniting. She looked at him, her radiant smile sending warmth throughout him, strong enough to withstand the worst Winter weather.

With Elizabeth and Georgiana accompanying him, one on each arm, he led them up the stairs. There was still part of the evening that concerned him, and that was Mrs. Bennet. She was an inveterate gossip and not a quiet one either. The evening could be ruined if she mentioned anything about Lydia's wedding. And with Georgiana on his other arm, he could not ask Elizabeth if her mother understood she needed to stay silent on the matter.

After entering Pemberley, his fears diminished when he did not hear Mrs. Bennet's voice. The entire Bennet family seemed to have been rendered speechless at his home's grandeur. For Mrs. Bennet's silence, he had never been more grateful for his wealth at that moment.

Miss Bingley, Mr. and Mrs. Hurst, who had been waiting in the sitting room, stood at their entrance. All professed eagerness to reconnect, even Miss Bingley, though it was uttered in quite a muted manner.

The Gardiners, Elizabeth, Georgiana, and Mr. Darcy, sat together in the ample seating area. In contrast, Jane and Mr. Bingley sat across each other in smaller chairs a few feet away. Their joy was clear to see; he could not deny it.

The rest of their group happily discussed their favorite parts of Derbyshire. Mr. Bennet was occupied with a book he found on a side table. Mrs.

Bennet and her daughters were most likely too over-whelmed yet to join in the conversation.

During a lull, Miss Bingley spoke up. "Pray, Miss Eliza, are the militia still quartered at Meryton?"

Mr. Darcy shot the woman a level stare which she did not notice, nor did her sister, who covered her mouth with her hand.

"No, they are encamped at Brighton for the summer."

He shifted in his seat and glanced at Mrs. Bennet with worry. This would be ideal for Mrs. Bennet to speak up about her youngest daughter's recent wedding.

"That must be a great loss for your family."

"We are bearing it as best we can, Miss Bingley."

Thankfully, Georgiana showed no signs of under-standing Miss Bingley and Elizabeth's conversation. However, if it persisted, he would have to do something.

"I should have thought one gentleman's absence might have caused particular pangs."

He gathered himself on the couch, ready to intervene. He trusted Elizabeth enough to know she would not say anything improper, but he did not trust Mrs. Bennet.

"I cannot imagine who you mean."

"I understood that certain ladies found the society of—"

"Oh!" Elizabeth abruptly stood. "How clumsy of me! I have spilled my lemon water all over my dress."

Mr. Darcy stared at the coincidence of Elizabeth spilling her drink at the perfect moment. But he should have known she would have had matters well in hand, though at a sacrifice to her comfort and reputation.

The gentlemen present hastened to provide handkerchiefs for Elizabeth to blot her dress.

"Oh, Lizzy, how could you? You will have to return to the inn to change," said Mrs. Bennet. "You cannot dine in a wet dress, though I will not be leaving to accompany you. One of your sisters will have to do it."

Elizabeth paused her blotting to glance at her mother. At that moment, a footman entered, announcing supper was ready. Mrs. Bennet was saved from hearing his thoughts about her willingness to force his betrothed from his home to change at the inn, which would take at least two hours.

He spun away, rolled his eyes, and then escorted his sister and Elizabeth into the dining room. Miss Bingley and the Hursts were the last to enter and sat farthest from him, which did not trouble him one wit. Mr. Bingley did not even notice, so enraptured by Jane, was he. The meal passed in good conversation except for Mrs. Bennet's interjections, which showed her poor grasp of the topic they were discussing.

When all eyes were on Mr. Bingley as he told a funny story, Mr. Darcy reached across the table and grasped Elizabeth's hand. She squeezed back with a warm smile, and he got lost in her eyes until she had to turn her head to answer a question.

He glanced at his sister, who thankfully had no idea of what had almost transpired in the sitting room. If he could, he would keep knowledge of Wickham as her brother-in-law from her forever.

After supper, Mr. Darcy broke tradition and had the men join the women immediately. He was loath to leave them alone for fear of what Miss Bingley or Mrs. Bennet would say. Perhaps he was too protective of his sister. Still, he also knew Miss Bingley's nature had turned more caustic since Lady Catherine's visit. He did not want her trying to corner Elizabeth. Or saying anything that would upset his sister or disclose the youngest Bennet daughter had not been wed to Wickham until quite recently.

A game of charades was quickly settled upon, but Miss Bingley pleaded an aching head and departed. The Hursts followed soon after once Mr. Hurst learned no one was interested in playing cards that evening. The rest had a delightful time with charades, and Mrs. Bennet's conjectures regarding the game did not spoil the mood. The evening ended with a singing and piano performance by Georgiana, Mary, and Elizabeth.

Mr. Darcy finally had time alone with Elizabeth when he escorted her down the front steps to their waiting carriage. "I must thank you for spilling your drink earlier at a most opportune moment."

"I do not know what you mean, Mr. Darcy? I am naturally clumsy." Elizabeth's mirthful eyes met his, and no more could be said, for they were quickly joined by the rest of the Bennet family.

He watched the carriages roll down the drive and out of sight, accompanied by Mr. Bingley. His friend stared with such a look of abject longing Mr. Darcy knew without a doubt that Jane would be engaged very soon.

CHAPTER 18

*E*lizabeth woke with a grin on her face. Nothing could ruin this day, not even rain, and from her view of the window from the bed, it looked like a splendid day. Jane was in high spirits, her mother had conducted herself well at Pemberley, and she was to wed a most congenial man.

She prepared for the day and encountered Jane in the hallway heading downstairs to break her fast. Elizabeth slipped her arm through Jane's. "How are you this morning?"

Jane gave a placid smile, then turned to the staircase. "I know what you are thinking, Lizzy, but I do not anticipate any address from Mr. Bingley."

Elizabeth jauntily tilted her head. "You might not anticipate any, but that does not mean the gentleman in question is not disposed to deliver them."

Jane glanced at her sister with an admonishing look. "Lizzy, I know you are overjoyed that I have renewed my acquaintance with Mr. Bingley, but I have learned to protect my heart around him."

Her happy mood dimmed at those words. "Protect your heart? Jane, you have never stopped thinking about him. You have not been yourself ever since he left Netherfield for London."

Now having descended the steps, Jane removed her arm from Elizabeth's. "He is the most affable man I have ever met, but now that he has renewed his acquaintance, will he return to London? No, Lizzy, it will be pleasant to converse with such an affable man, but I will return to Hertfordshire."

Elizabeth had not expected this reaction from her sister. How could Jane not see how sorrowful she had been since Bingley had quit Netherfield? She entered their private sitting room, intent on informing Jane of those facts but changed her mind when she saw their parents were already present.

LADY CATHERINE DE BOURGH narrowed her eyes as she glared out the carriage window. That obstinate, headstrong girl would not get the better of her. No, she would see to that upstart. No one would take what was her daughter's.

The well-appointed carriage pulled to a stop in front of the Lambton Parsonage. The door opened swiftly, and steps were deployed for her ladyship to descend to the drive. With her cane tapping along the gravel, Lady Catherine strode to the front door, where one of her tigers rapped at the door.

An older woman opened the door, straightening up after seeing the elegantly dressed woman of means in front of her.

"The housekeeper, I presume? Inform the parson that Lady Catherine de Bourgh is calling."

After curtsying, the housekeeper quickly retreated, wringing her hands as the great woman entered the small cottage, glanced around, then fixed her gaze on the housekeeper.

"Where is he? I have serious matters to address."

The housekeeper swallowed. "I shall—"

"Your ladyship, I was not expecting you." A severe looking, slightly older man with wispy black hair not entirely covering his head entered the main room. "I trust you remember the location of my study." He turned to the housekeeper. "Mrs. Giles, please bring us tea."

Then he hastened down a short hallway to his cramped study where he had been preparing a sermon. After a pause, in which Lady Catherine's lips pursed at the lack of deference, she pounded her cane on the wooden floor as she followed the man but stopped at the threshold of his study.

The small room had not changed much since her last visit. It was still brimming with books, with barely enough room for the pastor to squeeze past all the overflowing bookshelves to sit behind his desk covered with paper. Two plain wood chairs were in front of the desk, nearly at the edge of the room.

"These chairs look decidedly uncomfortable. I shall stand."

The parson blinked.

"Have you forgotten the promise you made to me? When I saved you from a life of destitution by recommending you for this living? The contract you signed?" Lady Catherine de Bourgh fixed the pastor with a steely glare. "I have received word that the Banns of Matrimony have been read for my nephew, Mr. Fitzwilliam Darcy, and a Miss Elizabeth Bennet."

The pastor stammered, "I—I—"

"This woman cannot be allowed to marry my nephew!"

"My lady, I understand, but," Mr. Woodforde stammered. "Do not hold me responsible if he refuses to listen to reason. I can only do my best to fulfill my obligation to you."

She narrowed her eyes. "Need I remind you of the contract terms you willingly, and might I remind you, gratefully signed?"

"I understand your concern," the pastor said cautiously. "But I must remind you that my parents are deceased, and my younger siblings are all grown now and no longer need my financial assistance. I must do as my patron—"

Lady Catherine de Bourgh stepped closer to the desk, the crack of her cane on the bare wooden floor reverberating like a musket shot. "Is not your brother Peter, a steward of the Chiltern Hundreds?" The pastor paled. "Your nieces and nephews many? They may not need your assistance so desperately now, but with a well-placed word from a noblewoman, they may be in dire straits."

Mr. Woodforde opened and closed his mouth but could not get any words out.

Lady Catherine arched an eyebrow. "I see I have made my wishes clear." She tapped the paper on his desk with her cane. "If you do not wish to suffer the consequences of my disappointment, I suggest you refuse to marry my nephew to that upstart gel and dissuade him from her."

The parson, hunched in his chair, his voice trembling, hesitantly broached the silence. "I beg your pardon, please, but I have met Miss Bennet and am hard-pressed to find any possible reason I could use. She is an exemplary gentlewoman."

"Do you know that gel's family? Her youngest sister, Lydia Bennet, recently eloped with an officer you must have heard of as he is from this area and turned out quite wild, a Mr. George Wickham."

The person stilled. "Wickham? George Wickham? I just married a George Wickham and Lydia Bennet, sister of Elizabeth Bennet, in my church."

Lady Catherine's stiff stance loosened as her head flinched back. "That cannot be so! I received word that Lydia Bennet had run away with George Wickham in the middle of the night. They were headed to Derbyshire, where he was raised." She narrowed her gaze on the parson once again. "Be it no matter, even if they are married now, she ran away with Wickham. Would you allow that woman's sister to marry into the Darcy family?"

Mr. Woodforde had been sorting through the many papers covering his desk when he pulled one sheet and held it up. "Here it is, the marriage certificate for Mr. George Wickham of Lambton, Derbyshire, and Miss Lydia Bennet of Meryton, Hertfordshire."

Lady Catherine snatched the paper from his hands, studying it. "They did not elope? It must have been a seven-night at the very least since they fled Brighton together!" She flung the paper back onto the desk, missing the parson's outstretched hand. "And this is the kind of family that you would associate forever more with the Darcy name? There is your reason to refuse this unholy alliance. Her family concealed this from you, a grave omission that Lydia Bennet had run away with Wickham yet were not wed!"

The parson's lips were so tightly pressed together they were almost white. He stood slowly, fury evident on his face. "I have been terribly betrayed. Mr. Bennet gave no indication of this." He closed his eyes and took a deep breath, visibly bracing himself, before opening them again. "I will put a stop to this immediately."

Lady Catherine de Bourgh nodded, then whirled around, leaving the cramped study before allowing her self-satisfaction to show on her face. She passed the housekeeper carrying the tea tray, who stopped in the small sitting room and watched the noble-woman exit the small parsonage.

Her ladyship climbed into her carriage and settled back on the bench with relief and a great sense of accomplishment. Her nephew was safe, and her daughter would marry him soon.

She would guarantee it.

"Oh Jane, my dearest child, come sit by me," implored Mrs. Bennet in the private sitting room at the Lambton Inn. "We must discuss what you will wear today. I am sure Mr. Bingley will call upon you, and you must look your best, for I am sure he is falling in love with you again!"

Elizabeth sighed as she settled at the table with the Gardiners.

"Now you must don your finest dress, the rose one. It brings out your complexion. I will have the maid pay special attention to your hair. Oh, if only she knew the latest styles from London, but I am not sure she knows any better. We will have to make do—"

"Sister," interjected Mr. Gardiner. "Let the girl eat."

Miss Bennet glanced askance at the other table. "You do not have four daughters to marry off. Your children are still young. You do not know how my nerves have suffered over the years worrying about my daughters' futures."

Elizabeth sipped her tea, and her appetite nearly vanished at the display from her mother. She looked to her father for help, but he was engrossed in *The Sun* folded on the table next to his plate.

"Mama," said Jane, "all of my dresses look fine. I will not choose to wear one specifically for Mr. Bingley."

"Oh, do not say such things, Jane! Of course, you will dress your best for Mr. Bingley. I find the rose one complements your eyes, but what is his favorite color? Perhaps the green would be most suitable?"

Elizabeth's thoughts turned as she tried to grasp another topic she could bring up to stop this ridiculous conversation, but Kitty prompted a new idea first. "Are you going to have an engagement ball, Lizzy?"

Mrs. Bennet's head turned towards Elizabeth's table, her face alight with excitement. "A ball! Yes, yes, you must have an engagement ball, and Jane will dance with Mr. Bingley, and then he will request her hand!"

Elizabeth groaned and gazed up at the ceiling.

"We must have new dresses. You cannot go to a ball at Pemberley in the worn dresses you have. I believe Mr. Bingley has seen you in every dress you have brought to Derbyshire. We will go to the modiste…

does Lambton have a modiste?" Mrs. Bennet leaned over the table to address Mrs. Gardiner.

She had to act. Her mother was quickly getting out of control. Elizabeth did not dare look at her aunt, who grew up in Lambton and cherished the little town dearly. "Mama, there is not a ball scheduled. We cannot order new dresses for a ball we do not know will even occur."

Mrs. Bennet waved a hand in the air. "Oh, Lizzy, stop your naysaying. Of course, Mr. Darcy will have a ball. He can well afford it with £10,000 a year!"

Elizabeth closed her eyes and raised a hand to her forehead. Her mother was going to be more insufferable than she already was. She would be very fortunate if Mr. Darcy did not decide to call off the wedding because of her mother's improper behavior. The same inappropriate behavior Mr. Darcy noted during his first terrible proposal in Hunsford.

She endeavored to focus on her breakfast while Mr. Gardiner pleaded with his sister to see reason when a serving maid knocked on their private sitting room door. "Pardon me. The parson is here to see you, sir."

Mr. Bennet quizzically peered at the maid over his spectacles. "Well, send him in."

The rest of the room's occupants shared inquisitive and puzzled glances at the visit from the parson. They had just seen him at Lydia and Wickham's wedding.

The elderly man, robed in his parson's cloak and hat, appeared quite severe and did not return Mr. Bennet's greeting. "Good morning, Mr. Woodforde. Come join us and—"

"I am here on grave business; I am sorry to inform you. I must speak with you, Mr. Bennet."

Elizabeth grabbed Jane's hand and had the short-lived worry that Mr. Darcy was calling off their wedding. But that was ridiculous as he was very much in love with her. But why else would the parson be visiting with serious news?

Mr. Bennet stood, wiping his mouth with the serviette. He motioned to the corner of the room, the only area not occupied.

"I insist we go somewhere private, Mr. Bennet."

That statement further heightened the misgivings Elizabeth was feeling into something resembling alarm.

"Is something the matter with my youngest, Lydia? Surely if there had been an accident, they would have—"

"Oh, my dearest Lydia! And she just got married too!" Mrs. Bennet's cry nearly drowned out Mr. Woodforde's response.

"This matter is not directly related to the youngest daughter *I recently wed*." The parson's emphasis deepened Elizabeth's misgivings. "But your actions regarding that matter have influenced me now."

"Against Lizzy?" Mr. Bennet stared at his favorite daughter, then looked back at the parson. "She has always been a model of propriety. No accusation has merit. What is this accusation, and who brought it to you?"

"This needs must be a private conversation, Mr. Bennet." The parson looked more severe.

All eyes were still on Elizabeth, who could scarcely believe what she was hearing.

Mr. Bennet waved his hand. "There is nothing that could possibly have any truth to it." Then he paused and raised his eyebrows. "Do not tell me you heard of this accusation from a Lady Catherine de Bourgh?"

Elizabeth's eyes darted to the parson, who nodded.

"Indeed, you deceived me most appallingly regarding the nature of the relationship between your daughter Lydia and Mr. Wickham. They both fled together from Brighton, he deserting his commission, and they were not married! You concealed from the good people of Lambton and me that your daughter had been living with a man, unwed!"

Elizabeth's mouth dropped open, and gasps filled the deafening silence. Their attempt to contain Lydia's destructive actions was all for naught. With the parson, this angered; there was no telling who he would tell, and her family's reputation would be ruined.

If the outcry was loud enough, would Mr. Darcy have no choice but to end their engagement?

"If there was deception involving one daughter, then it stands to reason there would be deception with another." He motioned to the table where Elizabeth sat, her jaw agape.

Mr. Gardiner stood, his chair scraping against the bare wood of the floor. "Come now, there was no need to speak of my niece in that fashion. That was uncalled for. She has always been a model of propriety. Your accusation has no merit whatsoever."

"Then you deny that you have duped me regarding your youngest daughter? That she had run away with a man, yet never married until I conducted the service for whom I thought were good, God-fearing people?" Mr. Woodforde's serious gaze settled again on Mr. Bennet.

"Would the outcome have changed in any manner if you had known that detail?" asked Mr. Bennet. "Wickham procured a special license from the Bishop. Is that not sufficient?"

The parson continued as if Mr. Bennet had not even uttered a word. "I will not be deceived again. What trouble does this other daughter of yours bring? No, I cannot condone this wedding in my church. I have served the parish of Lambton and am well acquainted with the Darcy family. On her deathbed,

I promised the late Mrs. Darcy I would watch over her son."

In the gaping silence of the poleaxed assemblage, the parson stormed out of the private sitting room, slamming the door behind him.

Elizabeth thought it sounded remarkably like the doors of the church slamming closed in front of her, not allowing her entrance. Suddenly the room erupted in the sudden cacophony of people speaking at once, Mrs. Bennet wailing and chairs scraping against the wooden floor.

Jane wrapped an arm around her shoulders. Mrs. Gardiner grasped one of her hands. "This will not stand, Lizzy. I am sure of it. I know how much that young man is in love with you, and I doubt this will stop anything. Do not worry, you will see. All will be right."

But she could not speak or even seem to turn her head. Jane squeezed her other hand. "Lizzy, our aunt, is correct. This is a desperate last-ditch effort by Lady Catherine de Bourgh to prevent the wedding. Mr. Darcy will not allow that to happen. I have no doubt at all in the matter."

Elizabeth gulped air and pulled her hands out of their holds. "I cannot breathe. I need to get some air."

"Jane, can you accompany her? I need to help calm down your mother."

She did not recall how she ended up outside with her jacket, bonnet, and walking boots. It had been a blur of wiping tears. Jane had taken care of her like she was a young child. But now, out of the small town on the road, she felt more herself. Most likely because no one was staring at her.

But she could not shake the complete sincerity the parson had uttered the damning words. As if a wealthy noblewoman could have informed the man of the cloth of nothing but the absolute truth when Elizabeth knew it was the farthest from it.

CHAPTER 19

Mr. Darcy leaned back in his chair, stretching his arms over his head and arching his back with a sigh. He had been determined to finish his correspondence. He wished to call upon Elizabeth without any thoughts of business that needed to be taken care of. And he could not think of any business he had missed that would require the parson calling at Pemberley.

Mr. Darcy stood as the parson entered his study.

"I am afraid I am bringing bad news, Mr. Darcy. May I sit?"

Mr. Darcy motioned toward one of the chairs in front of his desk. The parson settled as Mr. Darcy lowered himself in his chair with dread. Had Eliza-

beth changed her mind and canceled their engagement? But he could not fathom such an action, as
she seemed very much in love with him. It was also
far more to her and her family's benefit to continue
with the wedding. His reputation would survive the
wedding being called off, but hers would not.

"Your aunt, Lady Catherine de Bourgh, came to me
with serious accusations against your intended, but
in the discussion, I learned the news of an even more
alarming nature. In the interest of the Darcy name
and your family's reputation, I will not preside over
a wedding to another Bennet daughter."

Mr. Darcy's fingers clenched the wooden and leather
arms of his desk chair. He should have known when
she departed Pemberley far too quickly. Would her
poisonous tongue ever stop? "And what were the
alarming news and the charges my aunt leveled
against my intended?"

The parson seemed flustered at the equanimity of
Mr. Darcy's response. "That your engagement is
false as you are engaged to her daughter, Anne de
Bourgh. But most importantly, I was also deceived
most horribly by the Bennet family regarding the
nature of their youngest daughter, Lydia Bennet's,
relationship with George Wickham."

When the parson did not continue, Mr. Darcy narrowed his eyes. "Is that it?"

The parson blinked, then gathered himself as his duty to the young man of his parsonage, the same man that owned his living, was not yet done. "I was led to believe they had married in Scotland in that pagan custom of handfasting, which is an affront to God, but the truth is even worse. They had not wed at all! They lived as husband and wife for at least a seven-night before the wedding!" The parson had stiffened while speaking; such was his outrage.

Mr. Darcy stared at the man. "Those are two separate issues, not at all connected. My aunt has persisted with this idea that my mother and she planned an engagement of myself with her daughter. Allegedly when my cousin was still in the crib. However, my mother never mentioned it. Indeed, it was only after her passing that Lady Catherine voiced this arrangement. As to the second accusation, did Wickham not have a special license from the Bishop?"

"The Bishop was obviously not aware of the nature of the Bennet girl."

"Would that have made a difference? Compromised couples have wed with special licenses before."

The parson frowned and studied Mr. Darcy. "The deception, the concealment of the true nature of their relationship to me, a man of God, shows a distinct lack of concern for propriety and comportment."

Mr. Darcy studied the older man he had known as his parson for his entire life. He had always considered the man of a serious but genial nature. However, his sentiments against the Bennet family's concealment, which was not unfounded, did not lie well with Mr. Darcy. "And how do you think they obtained access to a special license?"

"Well, Mr. Wickham went and…er…."

"Does that not demonstrate that he planned to wed Lydia Bennet?"

"But that still does not signify the deception and concealment of the character of—"

"I accompanied Wickham to London when he obtained a special license from the bishop, who approved and granted Wickham's request. And I also purchased a special license to wed Elizabeth Bennet."

He paused, enjoying the surprise on the parson's face, but it did not wipe away his ire at the man. "For you see, we were also compromised."

The parson gasped.

"By my sheep who knocked Miss Bennet and me into the lake at Pemberley."

Mr. Darcy abruptly stood, pushing his chair back silently on the thick rug. "I do not want to hear any more besmirching of Miss Bennet's or the Bennet family's reputation."

The parson's mouth moved, perhaps an apology, but no sounds were uttered. Mr. Darcy walked around his desk and opened the door.

"I can assure you, Mr. Woodforde, that Miss Elizabeth Bennet is the most upstanding gentlewoman I have ever encountered."

The parson collected his hat and stood, but Mr. Darcy raised a hand to impede any further discourse on the subject.

"I will marry Miss Elizabeth Bennet, but I will certainly not have you as the officiant, per your desires. You are dismissed."

After the parson hastened out of the room, Mr. Darcy slammed the door behind him with more force than necessary.

But then he flung open the door and sprinted down the hall, quickly catching up to the older parson. "Did you come to me directly with this information, or did you inform anyone else?"

The parson halted and turned to him, his hands gripping the edge of his cloak. "I had to inform the woman's family that there would not be a wedding."

Mr. Darcy shut his eyes and ran a hand over his face. Then dashed past the man while shouting for his horse to be readied immediately.

HE SPURRED his horse faster at spying the outer buildings of Lambton. He would arrive flushed and coated in dust, but he could not have waited for a carriage to be readied. And he knew Elizabeth would not mind the state of his clothing. Just the thought of her stricken face had him yelling at his horse to gallop faster.

A cloud of dust enveloped him at the horse's abrupt stop in front of the inn. He tossed the reins to the nearest stable, then rushed inside the inn.

"I must speak with Miss Elizabeth Bennet." He slapped his hat against his leg.

A throat cleared behind him, and he turned to find her father. "Lizzy is out walking with her sister, Jane. We received an unexpected visit from the parson this morning."

Mr. Darcy tightened his lips. "He also just called on me. I hastened here straight away. Where did they walk? I must inform her that the parson is mistaken. Nothing has been canceled. We are still betrothed."

Mr. Bennet pursed his lips and clasped his hands behind his back. "I must ask you how this wedding will take place if the parson does not marry you in the local church?"

"There are two livings that I am the patron of. Kympton is the other. Miss Bennet and I will wed there."

Mr. Bennet cleared his throat. "I see. Very well, I know they had decided to walk on the outskirts of town to avoid most of the populace. I do not know exactly where they went. If you pardon me, I have to deliver the good news to my wife, who, as you can imagine, has been affected greatly by this news."

Mr. Darcy hurried out the door taking the reins back from the stable lad and mounting Caesar. He could cover ground faster on horseback, which he did but at a brisk trot so as not to miss any sign of her. Knowing how much Elizabeth liked to walk on country lanes, he took the closest road out of Lambton near the inn and found her and Jane not far out of town walking along the packed dirt road.

"Elizabeth!"

At his call, the two sisters stopped and turned. As he rode closer, he spied that the parson's words had greatly afflicted her. Mr. Darcy wished a pox of a thousand boils on that man.

He leaped down from his horse and took her hands in his. "The parson just visited me. I must apologize for my aunt has meddled." Elizabeth sniffed. "But rest assured, our wedding will still take place far sooner than waiting for the rest of the Banns to be read. I also procured a special license in London, and we can be wed tomorrow in Kympton."

Elizabeth's face, at first stricken and pale, was now lit with joy. She raced to him, holding out her hands. He squeezed her hands, relieved that his aunt had not scared her off.

"Oh, Fitzwilliam!"

He breathed deeply of her particular scent and gazed at her tear-stained face. "I apologize again, profusely, for what my aunt has done. Surely, you could not have thought I would have been so easily deterred from marrying you?"

Elizabeth laughed. "No, I knew of your affection for me. But I also know how much power your aunt wields. You said we would wed tomorrow in Kympton?"

"I think it best to wed as quickly as possible. My aunt will not give up easily. I underestimated her resolve, but I will not do so again."

"The parson will still not officiate our wedding?"

Mr. Darcy saw his intended's concerned features, and his anger rose again. "I did not give him the option."

Elizabeth studied him. "You are not considering his dismissal from the living at Lambton?"

Her compassion for the parson that had caused her so much distress was admirable and was one of her many fine features that he admired. "I confess, I had been."

She bit her lip, her eyes wandering over his face. "I would not wish him to lose this living over his fierce protection of your family's reputation. My youngest sister's thoughtlessness and my family's protection of our reputation put the parson in an unenviable position."

Mr. Darcy nodded, her request was sound, but he would decide upon the parson's living later. After they were wed. He turned to Jane, who was standing near Caesar, petting his neck. "I shall walk you back to the inn. I already informed your father, who was eager to share the news with your mother."

Elizabeth laughed as they turned to walk back to Lambton. "Yes, she will be quite delighted to know that our wedding will still occur."

She turned to Mr. Darcy. "You did not speak to my mother yourself?"

"I did not." He turned to look at her with a quizzical expression.

"Mama had it in her head that we must have an engagement ball. I am glad she did not bring it up. I was sure she would have accosted you at the first opportunity."

"You do not want an engagement ball? Though it would be a wedding ball after tomorrow. I recall you enjoyed dancing at the assemblies."

"I do love them, but I would not demand it of you. A ball requires planning and a fortnight of preparation."

"Not for me, it would not. A ball to announce our marriage would be a large enough spectacle, even if no invitations were issued to distant relatives, that Lady Catherine would be unable to continue her machinations." He caught her attention, looked at Jane, and then returned to his intended.

Elizabeth beamed and grasped his hand. "I think that is a wonderful idea, Fitzwilliam."

CHAPTER 20

*E*lizabeth watched her intended as he mounted Caesar and threw her a quick smile before galloping towards Kympton. With a nudge and a cry, the horse bounded into a fast trot, throwing up dust clouds in his passing.

"I am delighted everything has worked out for you, Lizzy," said Jane. "After the parson's visit, it seemed like your wedding would never take place. I am very ecstatic for you."

Elizabeth, her body still tingling from the extreme change in circumstances, could not stop grinning. "I can hardly believe it myself." She turned toward Jane with a mischievous look. "Until after our vows in front of the parson, I won't."

With both sisters beaming at each other and with buoyant steps, they entered the inn arm in arm and proceeded down the hallway to the private sitting room. Unfortunately, Mrs. Bennet's piercing voice carried far enough to be heard in the hallway. After a quick glance at Jane, Elizabeth opened the door.

"—must have them! How can we wear dresses we have already worn to Lydia's wedding? We must have new dresses for the wedding—"

"Mama," exclaimed Elizabeth. "Please, lower your voice. We could hear you in the hallway."

"Nonsense, I doubt anyone could hear anything, what with all the people coming and going. I have never been in an inn so raucous." Mrs. Bennet flicked her handkerchief.

Mary closed her book. "We have not ventured such a distance before without relations nearby. This is our first stay at an inn, thus—"

"Oh, Mary! Do you forget your parent's wedding holiday? We traveled to Brighton and stayed at the inn not far from the ocean. The inn was capacious and quite elegant, right on the promenade."

Elizabeth sat down at the table and poured herself a cup of tea. The news during breakfast had left her with no appetite, but now after being reassured by Mr. Darcy, she was quite famished.

"Is the news not wonderful, Lizzy?" asked Mrs. Bennet. "I would have thought you would be over-joyed with excitement. I know I was the day before I married Mr. Bennet. My poor nerves could barely contain it." Mrs. Bennet glanced at Elizabeth calmly, drinking tea. "I would be unable to eat with having my wedding postponed, then arranged for the very next day—"

Elizabeth paused in the motion of bringing her teacup to her mouth. "Tomorrow?"

"—and of course, I had asked Mr. Bennet for dresses for your wedding. But he obstinately refused to be kind, and now we shall have no new—"

She slowly set her cup back down on the saucer.

"Lizzy? What is wrong?" Jane leaned over and squeezed Elizabeth's hand.

Elizabeth looked around the room, the rest of her family staring at her. "Tomorrow is quite abrupt."

Mr. Bennet lowered the newspaper he had been reading to stare directly at her. "Indeed, and that was why your intended thought it imperative to wed on the morrow, so his aunt could no longer interfere. She will be expecting two more weeks of the Banns read."

Mrs. Bennet stared at Elizabeth as if she was irrational. "Of course, it is tomorrow! Mr. Darcy informed Mr. Bennet of that, which Kitty heard, and dashed upstairs to tell me! I had to recline. No one knows what I suffer with my nerves. How dreadful for someone of the cloth to behave in such a manner!"

She knew Mr. Darcy had informed her of the change in their wedding date, yet the news had not fully registered until this very moment. There was a valid reason for advancing the wedding date by a fortnight, but she had not been prepared for this to be her last day with her family.

Her eyes swept one by one to her family members scattered throughout the room. Kitty looked down at the floor, listening to Mary reading by the fire. Jane leaned towards Lizzy staring with concern as their mother described the extravagances she expected Mr. Darcy's estate to have but that she had not seen during her previous visit. Mr. Bennet read the newspaper.

"Lizzy?"

She turned to Kitty.

"Did you ask Mr. Darcy if there will be an engagement ball?"

"Oh, Kitty, stop pestering us about a ball! It is not as if you expect to meet your beau at it," Mrs. Bennet snapped.

Kitty slumped down in her lap. Elizabeth glared at her mother with disapproval. Had Mrs. Bennet not noticed how despondent Kitty had been since Lydia had departed?

Mrs. Bennet turned towards her least favorite daughter. "You *must* have a ball. The Lucases did not have one for Charlotte, and rightly so, for *I* would not want to celebrate a marriage that would rob my daughter of her home!" Elizabeth sighed while Jane squeezed her hand. "But a wedding ball at Pemberley will be quite the event. I dare say the Lucases, even though William is knighted now, would have a hard time—"

Elizabeth erupted with laughter.

Mrs. Bennet was not amused. "Lizzy! It is not lady-like to laugh boisterously! And at nothing to boot! You will be hauled off to Bedlam if you do not stop."

"Mr. Darcy's estate is not Pebbly," Kitty announced. "But *Pemberley*."

"I did not say Pebbly! How could you accuse me of such a thing? I have a notion—"

Jane tugged at her hand. "Come, Lizzy. Let us go upstairs. I am unsure which dress to wear. I wish I had brought more, but I had expected only one wedding to attend."

She stood following Jane but stopped to pat Kitty on the shoulder. "Yes, Kitty, I did ask him, and he thought it a marvelous idea. There will be a wedding ball, and you," she tapped her sister's shoulder, "are very much expected to attend and dance as much as you can!"

With Kitty's spirits restored, and a smile on Elizabeth's face at the transformation, she followed Jane out of the room, glad to escape Mrs. Bennet's enthusiastic demands for dresses from Mr. Bennet.

IN THE CRAMPED room they now shared upstairs in the inn, Jane unpacked her dresses and laid them on the bed. "I wore this one to Lydia's wedding. It is the nicest dress I brought with me, but I do not feel I should flaunt it at both weddings."

"The only ones that will notice are the same people who attended Lydia's wedding, and we are all wearing the same clothes again for my wedding." She paused, a blush rushing through her that she was getting married tomorrow. "There is not enough time to make a new dress, even if Papa would agree to it."

Jane lowered the blue dress and studied her sister. "You know he would, Lizzy. But, I cannot conceive of the modiste in Lambton having a dress ready for you by early morning tomorrow."

Elizabeth shook her head and considered her dresses one by one. "I cannot fathom how much this is costing for our family to stay at this inn this long. We are perpetually short on funds, as Mama reminds us often."

"It is your wedding day. I think you should have a new dress." She motioned to the dress Elizabeth held in her hands. "Have you not patched that dress and covered it with ribbon several times already?"

Nodding, Elizabeth fixed her gaze on the barely disguised worn hem she had attempted to hide with ribbons. "I do not know what the parson will think when he sees me in this dress. He will think I accepted Mr. Darcy for his wealth."

Jane pursed her lips, an unusual display for her. "I was quite astonished at what Mr. Woodforde said. I could not have imagined any man of the cloth thinking so ill of our family."

"I can when Lady Catherine de Bourgh has his ear."

"What do you expect will happen to him? I cannot envision he thought it sensible to halt the wedding of his patron."

Elizabeth shook her head as she perched on the bed." Neither can I. He must have assumed Mr. Darcy would be grateful for his interference, for his effort to rescue him from marrying into our family."

Jane clenched her jaw, a rare display for her. "He uttered awful things, Lizzy. It is not true at all, you know."

"He was not wrong, though. We did conceal the nature of Lydia and Wickham's relationship."

Jane scowled. "But there was an excellent reason why we had to do so. The parson would have understood that any family with unmarried daughters would have done the same. Kitty and Mary have to be able to find suitable husbands."

Elizabeth swiveled and inspected her sister's face. "You do not consider yourself needing to find a husband? Have you already discovered one, then?" She teasingly smiled at her sister, who did not reciprocate it.

"I do not believe that I will ever love again. I will never find a man as wonderful as Mr. Bingley."

Elizabeth swiveled towards her with some measure of shock. "Jane, do you not think you will marry Mr. Bingley?" Jane looked at her hands in her lap. "He has not taken his eyes off you since he saw you again. I am certain he loved you then and loves you still."

"We have renewed our friendship, but that is all, Lizzy. I am convinced he will not offer for me." Jane bustled about putting her dresses back. "I hope Mama did not already send clothing to be laundered.

These dresses should be prepared by tomorrow morning if we dispatch them out now."

Elizabeth lifted her pale pink dress and chewed her bottom lip. She could not understand why Mr. Bingley had not proposed to her sister yet. It had been evident he was still in love with Jane.

Never would she have dreamed or wanted this for Jane, for Mr. Bingley and her to have rekindled their acquaintance but have nothing come of it. She would have to ask Mr. Darcy if there was anything he could do.

CHAPTER 21

*M*r. Darcy scowled at the countryside speeding past. He had been rash in deciding to go directly to Kympton. Caesar's hooves kicked up a cloud of dust, coating him in dirt. This was not his wisest move, but he felt too strongly about this errand to wait until returning home and sending a note to the parson at Kympton. Moreover, it was essential that he personally handle it.

The church spire came into view through the trees, prompting him to urge Caesar to move faster. He was already thinking ahead of all that needed to be undertaken before the next day. His cook, the house-keeper, and the valet would need to be informed of his upcoming wedding, but that news would have to be concealed from everyone else. He could not let anything reach his aunt ahead of time, as he was quite positive she had a source of news within Pemberley. Though he could not imagine who it could be. All his staff were loyal to him and had been with the Darcy family for at least a generation or two.

He slowed Caesar, then jumped down, walking him over to the well, pumping water into the pail for his horse to drink. After quenching his parched throat with a cup of water, he strode to the parsonage and knocked on the door, still clutching the reins.

No response came from inside, and Mr. Darcy frowned. Was the parson even home? Usually, he kept regular visiting hours, paying morning calls to parishioners and writing sermons in the afternoon. Where was Mr. Ahearn?

He sighed and raked his hand through his hair. What if the parson wasn't there? His worries were interrupted by a sound from within. Mr. Darcy pulled on Caesar's reins, but the horse wouldn't stop munching on the grass near the door. A tingle of panic ran up his spine when the door didn't open. "Mr. Ahearn? Are you in there? It is Mr. Darcy. I have an urgent matter to discuss with you."

He growled and pounded harder on the door. Indeed, if the man was in the back of the parsonage writing a sermon, he would surely hear him knocking. There was no reply, and Mr. Darcy shuffled, running his hand through his hair. To his astonishment, the door finally opened— "Good God, man!"

He stumbled back as his horse snorted, backing away. The parson looked gravely ill, coughing and doubling over. Mr. Darcy stepped further away, covering his mouth and nose with his arm. The poor man needed to be put back to bed. He felt like a villain for bothering the sick man.

"Where is your housekeeper? You must get back in bed! "

"She is fetching the physician." His statement was punctuated by another round of hacking.

"Please return to bed. You are very unwell. I will send servants to you. You should have sent a note!" Mr. Darcy retreated as the parson coughed again. "I will make sure the physician is on his way."

The parson nodded, then after coughing and leaning on the doorjamb, he peered up at his visitor. "What can I do for you, Mr. Darcy?"

"Never mind me. You're too ill. Please, go back to bed."

The parson tried to respond but was overcome with coughing and finally stepped back inside and shut the door. Mr. Darcy left the parsonage, craning his neck skyward while absently running his hand through his hair. How could the parson have become so dreadfully sick in summer? More importantly, what was he going to do about marrying Elizabeth tomorrow?

He lowered his arm and shook his head, all hope of their wedding tomorrow fading. Mr. Darcy hopped onto Caesar's back, turning him around and guiding him down the same road they had galloped, but at a much more leisurely pace. There was no point hurrying anymore since the wedding couldn't take place the next day.

As he rode, a cloud of dust grew on the horizon. Most likely a carriage or cart coming up the lane. He didn't quicken Caesar's pace. His horse trotted smoothly at a ground-eating speed. The dust resolved into a pony cart, and Mr. Darcy cursed when it drew closer. It was the last man he wanted to see. He clamped his lips together and glared, then slowed Ceasar to a halt as a disagreeable idea occurred to him.

Mr. Woodforde brought his pony to a halt. "Good day, Mr. Darcy. I am on my way to visit Mr. Ahearn. He is terribly ill. I have been helping Mrs. Shea nurse him these last several days."

"Yes, he is quite ill. I am shocked that I hadn't heard anything about it."

The parson looked up at Mr. Darcy. "He took ill suddenly after jumping into Bar Brook to save the Smith's youngest lad who fell in while fishing. Mr. Ahearn is an excellent swimmer but still caught a chill, and I fear he is very sick."

He commended the young boy for saving himself from the chill water. His housekeeper had called upon Mr. Darcy, desperately needing aid to care for Mr. Ahearn, who was far too ill. There were only two of them there.

Mr. Darcy steadied Caesar, chewing on his bit and shaking his head, and spoke. "The stream is quite enticing for young boys but prodigiously dangerous. I am sending servants to help Mrs. Shea care for him, but they will not arrive until late tonight."

"That is good of you." The awkward silence was broken by Mr. Woodforde. "Mr. Darcy, please, you must forgive me. I had no choice in the matter of what I did."

"You very much had a choice in the matter. But this matter has been decided already, and you are urgently needed by Mr. Ahearn." Mr. Darcy gathered the reins in preparation to rapidly depart.

"I must tell you what I have concealed. Mr. Ahearn may wait a moment or two because I must confess." Mr. Woodforde swallowed. "I had no choice, sir. Lady Catherine de Bourgh recommended me for the living at Lambton to your late father. She knew of my family and that we were in desperate straits with my father ill with a cough from working in the mines and seven mouths to feed. There was never enough." He swallowed again, looking down. "Lady Catherine knew of our situation, we were on Matlock land, and she offered the living to me, the oldest son. I could provide for my family, raise their fortunes, and care for my father. But—" Here, the parson paused as if gathering his resolve. "Her assistance was not entirely altruistic. I had to sign a contract to offer whatever assistance her ladyship needed for the rest of my life."

Mr. Darcy frowned. His aunt would not need assistance far removed from her residence.

"After I was settled at Lambton as the new parson, I discovered what kind of assistance she required."

The parson paused again. Mr. Darcy loathed hearing what the man would say next but could not turn away nor stop the man from speaking.

"She wanted me to ensure you married no one else but her daughter."

If Mr. Darcy stilled, staring at the parson. He tilted his head, unable to believe what he had heard.

Mr. Woodforde continued, "It was too late for me to refuse the living. I was installed in Lambton for nearly a year, my income flowing to my family. I was trapped, so I assented to her demand."

Mr. Darcy looked down without seeing the dirt road. He could not imagine the scenario, yet he could very well envision his aunt behaving that way. He raised his head towards the remorseful parson. "That was so long ago. She could not possibly have that hold over you now?"

The parson flushed and looked down as he spoke. "She reminded me that she could have me removed from the living at any time and easily be replaced. I understand she is on amicable terms with the Bishop. I am still supporting most all of my siblings and their families. If I was displaced, I could not let that happen."

"Why did you not tell me of this before now? My aunt may have tremendous influence but so do I as your patron."

"I did not want to admit something so disgraceful and embarrassing."

Mr. Darcy wanted to flee, far away from this man, but he looked aside and collected himself before turning back. "You believed what you said to me, though, regarding Miss Bennet and her family."

Mr. Woodforde rubbed his jaw. "I find her family's efforts to hide the truth of their daughter's situation disgraceful. But I did stir up my anger so I would be believed as to why the wedding could not proceed."

"And you did not inform me of my aunt's hold over you when calling upon me? You took it upon your-self to refuse to wed me to the woman I chose!"

"I could not, sir. I regretted what I did even as I did it."

Mr. Darcy could hear the anguish and misery in the man's voice, but he could not look at him anymore. He turned Caesar off the lane and around in a circle. He did know whether to pity the man or condemn him entirely.

"Sir, I am not positive what would have happened to me if I had not been lucky enough to be given a living. But I did everything possible to free myself of my dependence on her ladyship. Still, through my meager efforts, I could not devise a way to release my obligation to her."

"Did you receive recompense for your service to her?"

The parson shook his head. "No, sir. The only recompense is continuing to have the living at Lambton."

"Which was not even under her jurisdiction." Mr. Darcy had not known his aunt was as canny and manipulative as this. It boggled his mind that his aunt would threaten and control a man of the cloth, in his employ, to do her bidding as to whom he married. "I want you to say nothing of this revelation to my aunt. Behave as you have been, but anything Lady Catherine tells you to do, tell me. Though I cannot fathom she will stay in contact once she learns her attempts to force me to wed my cousin have failed." His horse was restless again. Mr. Darcy led Caesar in a circle before facing the parson once again. It had also given him time to settle his plans. "You will keep the living at Lambton. You will assist Mr. Ahearn in whatever capacity he needs while he recovers. And tomorrow morning, you will marry Elizabeth Bennet and me at Lambton."

The parson was effusive with his gratitude. He was nearly in tears. "Oh, thank you, thank you—"

Mr. Darcy cut him off with a wave of his hand. "I will inform the Bishop of your meritorious service to counteract anything my aunt endeavors. Eight o'clock tomorrow morning. Tell no one. This must be kept secret from my aunt. Now I must go."

He spurred Caesar into a gallop, drowning out anything the parson said. Time was of the essence; he had wedding preparations to arrange while keeping the entire event hidden.

CHAPTER 22

Mr. Darcy leaped off Caesar, tossing the reins to a waiting stable lad, then sprinted to his study where he hastily scrawled a note to Elizabeth. Hours had elapsed since he set off for Kympton, but he had apprised her of his intention to wed her tomorrow. The news that they were indeed marrying in the morning should not cause distress. She only had to appear at the appointed time.

After entrusting the note to a footman to ride swiftly to the Lambton Inn, Mr. Darcy raced upstairs, eager to cleanse the day's grime. At the top of the stairs, he encountered Miss Bingley standing on the mezzanine. He scowled at his uncouth behavior of running up the staircase. Still, Miss Bingley's opinion did not elicit any regret on his part.

"My goodness," she exclaimed. "You are in quite a flurry! Did your carriage break down? "

"Er, pardon me, I must—I have affairs to attend to. Excuse me." Without hesitating, he hastened down the hall to his room.

He yanked at his cravat while summoning his valet. So flustered at the necessity to hasten, he could not converse with his senior staff in this state. Yet, he knew they needed all the time they could get to prepare for his unanticipated wedding in the morning.

After a brisk bath and a clean set of clothing, he rushed to his study to meet with Mrs. Reynolds, his cook, and valet. He could not risk sharing the details with his valet outside his study. It was imperative his aunt not catch wind of his plans, and he did not know how she had been informed so accurately.

He strode into his study, closing the door behind him and speaking before he had even circled his desk to stand behind it. "I have news that must stay between those in this room. It cannot be divulged to anyone until after tomorrow morning."

He pinned each with his gaze, and all nodded in unison with nearly identical perplexed expressions. "Miss Elizabeth Bennet and I are to be married tomorrow morning. I will need a wedding breakfast for her family and the Gardiners, the same number as before."

"Sir," Mrs. Reynolds interjected, "your wedding, why can we not share the good news with the staff? I know we all have been waiting for the day to rejoice with good cheer."

"And the staff will rejoice, but not until after I am wed. My aunt, Lady Catherine de Bourgh, has been attempting to prevent my wedding to Miss Bennet. She wants me to marry her daughter and has been meddling with the Bennets and Mr. Woodforde." He nodded at their gasps. "If you see her or her staff, do not let them on the grounds and inform me immediately."

"Tomorrow? A wedding breakfast? Sir, I can't work miracles! I ask ye—" the cook began to complain.

"I understand, but do the best you can under the circumstances. I will approve all expenses and send out for what you need."

The housekeeper and cook exchanged looks of astonished delight. "Of course, Mr. Darcy," the housekeeper said. "We will do everything in our power. You can count on us to keep it a secret. I have a question, though. Your sister knows, of course?"

"No, I will tell her on the way to the church in the morning. Nothing can leak out, and my sister would be unable to contain her pleasure." After shocked glances between the staff, he continued. "I will need the mistress' room readied as well."

Mrs. Reynolds' mouth was nearly a perfect circle. "Sir, I will need the girls to help me ready the room. What reason shall I give them as to why we are readying the room?"

He shifted and looked down at his desk, unable to invent a reason to assuage the staff's curiosity.

"Should I tell them," the housekeeper continued, "it is being aired out so Miss Bennet may organize the room to her satisfaction before she resides at Pemberley?"

"Yes, that will do perfectly. Thank you. Now, let us get to work. We have much to do and very little time to do it in."

Mr. Darcy ascended the main staircase to speak to Georgiana. Still, she was not in her room, the music room, or the library. He eventually found her in the sitting room, but she was not alone. How would he tell her to be ready to go into town the next morning without arousing the suspicions of the Bingley sisters?

"Oh, Mr. Darcy! We have been eagerly awaiting you," Caroline greeted him from the card table where she sat with the Hursts and Mr. Bingley.

"Yes, you have had a stimulating day," exclaimed Mrs. Hurst.

Mr. Bingley laid down his cards and strode towards him. "You do not look worse for wear, though. Lucky that you were not seriously injured."

Georgiana sprang from the settee where she had been reading, paling as she hastened to hug her brother. "I was so worried!"

He stood stock still, blinking, then embraced his sniffling sister. "Hush, nothing is amiss. What do you think happened?"

Her words were so muffled against his coat that it was impossible to make anything out. Mrs. Hurst answered his query. "Why you were covered in dirt, head to toe, Caroline said!"

After a long look at Miss Bingley, he responded. "I had been riding when I received word the parson at Kympton was ill." He drolly added, "The roads are dusty."

Everyone spoke at once, glad that he was fine and not hurt. Mr. Bingley rebuked his sister for scaring them all. Georgiana did not leave his side, her arm wrapped around his as she reached up to wipe away her tears.

"This explains why I could not find you earlier," commented Mr. Bingley. "I wanted to ride into town."

Mr. Darcy led Georgiana to the sofa and sat. "Indeed, what business would you have in Lambton?"

"Well, I thought—call on Miss Bennet and—Darcy!" his friend spluttered.

Mr. Darcy grinned at his friend, a mischievous glint in his eye. "I am sorry, Bingley," he said, his tone light and teasing. "But I could not resist. Of course, I would happily join you in calling upon the Bennet sisters. In fact, I think it is a brilliant idea."

Mr. Bingley studied him. "You are in quite fine spirits! I cannot imagine being covered in dirt could fill you with delight. I know how fastidious you are."

He searched for some reason, as now even Georgiana was looking up at him in wonder. "Can I not be pleased to finally be home with my sister and good friend after a long day?"

"Friend? What about us?" Mrs. Hurst called out as she walked over from the card table. "Surely, you do not mean that we are not your friends?" She draped herself on a nearby settee, quickly joined by her sister.

"Not at all. But I was discussing the matter with Bingley. Therefore I only said friend in the singular. But you are very much my friends."

Louisa looked pleasingly at Caroline, but her sister continued to stare at Pemberley's owner with a forlorn yet desperate expression.

"Let us go first thing in the morning," stated Mr. Darcy, turning towards Mr. Bingley, "if you do not mind. I have some important business to attend to after that, and I do not want to be late."

Bingley agreed, and the two men made plans to call upon the Bennet girls early the next morning. Of course, he would inform his friend of the true nature of their calling upon the Bennet girls when the carriages arrived at the church.

"Oh, I should dearly love to call upon sweet Jane as well. Then stop at the shops—"

"How few there be," interjected Miss Bingley under her breath.

"—the quality of the gloves at the Milliner's quite surpassed my expectations. You would be surprised, Caro, by the quality of goods in this town."

Mr. Darcy blinked. This was an unexpected development, but it would work out well. Everyone currently residing at Pemberley would attend his wedding.

Georgiana turned to him, her arm still wrapped around his. "Oh brother, please, I would like to go as well!"

He looked down at his sister with raised eyebrows. "I believe it was understood you would accompany me to call upon Miss Elizabeth."

She squeezed his arm with a smile.

"Since we will have a large party, let us leave at half past seven. I do not want to be late."

All eyes focused on Mr. Darcy, then glances were exchanged among those on the settee. "Oh, well," said Mr. Bingley. "That is quite early, but certainly, with your business to attend to, we will be happy to accommodate you."

Murmurs from his sisters shared their agreement, though with less enthusiasm at the decidedly unusual early calling time.

They were then summoned to supper, which proceeded like other evenings before, except several times they had to repeat questions or statements to Mr. Darcy, who seemed to be uncharacteristically distracted.

Mr. Darcy nervously consulted his pocket watch as his valet presented him with various jackets. "Er, no, no, the blue one. Yes, that will do."

He had yearned for Elizabeth to be his wife, presiding over Pemberley as its mistress. Still, now that the day had finally arrived, he was more anxious than ever before in his life. After donning the jacket, he proffered his neck for the valet to tie his cravat. "Yes, very good."

Mr. Darcy hastened out of his bedroom, adjusting his sleeves which suddenly felt too tight. Then fiddling with his cravat. His valet must have tied it too tight. He bounded down the main staircase and entered the dining room, intent on consuming something even though the thought nauseated him.

Mr. Bingley was already present, nearly finished with his eggs. "You do not have to show me up so, Darcy. You have won your woman's affection!"

A smile that was more grimace greeted the observation.

"Are you unwell?" Mr. Bingley placed his teacup on the table.

"No, no, uh, I mean yes, perfectly well. Quite fine."

Mr. Darcy's denial did not have the intended effect as Mr. Bingley arched his eyebrows and gazed at his unusually nervous friend.

Georgiana entered the room then, providing a welcome distraction. Mr. Darcy excused himself to attend to some tasks, striding out, unaware of the two concerned glances. He sheltered in his study, pacing until finally, his pocket watch indicated it was time to depart.

Mr. Bingley and Georgiana were already gathered in the foyer, watching Miss Bingley and the Hursts descending the main staircase. The sisters were decidedly not at their usual best, looking discombobulated at the early hour. They entered two carriages, and after speaking in a muted voice to the driver of the Bingley carriage, Darcy clambered into his carriage with Georgiana already inside.

They were silent during the five-mile ride to Lambton. Mr. Darcy kept to his thoughts on his upcoming nuptials. Georgiana was not quite alert, but when they did not stop at the inn, she sat up and turned to her brother. "Where are we going? I thought we were to call upon Miss Elizabeth at the inn?"

He shifted on the carriage bench. "I may have lied, but for a good reason. Our aunt, Lady Catherine de Bourgh, has been causing trouble, trying to stop my wedding to Miss Elizabeth. So, we are on our way to the church for the wedding." At his sister's shocked expression, he chuckled. "I am afraid she is getting information somehow; therefore, I kept it a secret. Will you forgive me?"

Georgiana squealed with joy. She would have leaped out of her seat to hug Mr. Darcy, except for the carriage turning that moment onto the church's drive and rolling up next to the small stone church. They alighted quickly, Georgiana nearly skipping with exhilaration. Two carriages were parked, and the passengers were presumably already inside the church.

Mr. Bingley leaned his head out the carriage window. "Darcy, this is not the inn?"

A faint sound of sheep bleating reached him but was drowned out by Georgiana clapping her hands and bouncing on her feet. "Come inside! You must come inside!"

He stared at her curiously as the Bingley sisters leaned forward to look out the window, completely confused. Mr. Darcy cleared his throat, "Yes, please, there is something in the church to see first."

The Bingleys exited their carriage and quietly followed the Darcys into the church. Inside, they were very perplexed to see the Bennets and Gardiners turn around in the pews on the left side.

Then they noticed Mr. Bennet and Elizabeth standing to one side of the doors, a bouquet in her hands. Mrs. Hurst gasped as Caroline Bingley stupidly gawked.

Georgiana ran to Elizabeth, embracing her brother's intended in a tight hug before releasing her, still grinning.

The parson, standing on the altar with a bible, gestured to the right side of the church. "Please, come take your seats so the wedding may proceed."

aroline Bingley reeled back in shock, her pallid face twisted in horror. Mr. Bingley gripped her arm to steady her as she wavered. He offered Elizabeth an embarrassed grimace before leading his sister, aided by Mrs. Hurst, up the aisle. They took a seat in the pew on the right side, Mr. Hurst following, helping Caroline to settle.

Elizabeth's gaze was wrenched away from that spectacle as the Bingleys walked up the aisle, and she spotted the figure of Mr. Darcy standing on the other side of the doors. He pinned her with a gaze of both love and determination. Her nerves on her wedding day were calmed by a wave of warmth and happiness that washed over her when their eyes met.

When she had agreed to accompany her aunt and uncle on their holiday to the Peak District, Elizabeth never imagined it would end with her in love with Mr. Darcy, the very man she had detested upon first being introduced to him in Hertfordshire. Her heart swelled with love as she saw his smile meant only for her, then watched as he proudly escorted beaming Georgiana up the aisle. After his sister sat in the first pew, Mr. Darcy nodded to the parson before looking directly at Elizabeth.

Tingles raced over her skin as it was now her turn to walk up the aisle.

Mr. Bennet cleared his throat. "Well, Lizzy, let's not delay any longer."

She clasped his arm, and they slowly paced up the aisle, her eyes never leaving Mr. Darcy's. Elizabeth felt a rush of warmth at the sight of him, standing tall with a rigid posture, broad shoulders, and coat emphasizing his muscular form. Her heart pounded as his lips curved into a tender smile.

"My dearest Lizzy," Mr. Bennet quietly spoke. "Mr. Darcy is a remarkable gentleman, and I am proud to give you away to him. He is a man deeply in love with you, and I know you will be well cared for."

Elizabeth sniffled, biting the inside of her cheek to stop the tears threatening to fall. "I love you, Papa."

They stopped in front of Mr. Darcy, Mr. Bennet patting her hand resting on his arm as he addressed his soon-to-be son-in-law. "Take good care of my Lizzy."

Mr. Darcy solemnly nodded. "I plan to, sir."

Mr. Bennet extended his grasp of Elizabeth's hand to Mr. Darcy, who accepted it. Then Mr. Bennet stepped back, eyes glistening, but she was no longer looking at him. Elizabeth blinked ferociously to clear the moisture from her eyes, but it did not work very well. She turned to face the parson at her betrothed's side.

"Dearly beloved, we are gathered together here in the sight—"

She focused on breathing in and out, though her heart threatened to burst out of her chest.

"—the presence of God, and in the face of this company—"

The parson's voice ebbed into the background as she furtively glanced at Mr. Darcy to find that he was doing the same. He looked at her with such intensity and love she felt as though she were drowning.

"—if either of you knows any impediment, why ye may not be lawfully joined together in Matrimony, ye do now confess it—"

Elizabeth bit her bottom lip. While still quite sure that Lady Catherine had been avoided, she was still worried her ladyship had somehow discovered their wedding. She worried Mr. Darcy's aunt would suddenly barge into the church shouting that Elizabeth was stealing Mr. Darcy from her daughter, his rightful fiancé.

But she only heard the rustling of people, no angry accusations or objections. Elizabeth smiled, her breath coming quickly, her heart filled with happiness.

"Fitzwilliam Darcy, wilt thou have this woman to thy wedded wife—"

The parson droned on while she concentrated on standing upright, entirely in control of her faculties.

"I do." Mr. Darcy's voice was resolute.

She was not sure she was breathing.

"Elizabeth Bennet, wilt thou have this man to be thy wedded husband—"

Her eyes drifted to Mr. Darcy's hand, still grasping hers firmly. His fingers flexed, causing a jolt of energy to shoot through her body. She clutched his hand back tightly, unable to deny the urge to touch him.

"—and, forsaking all other, keep thee only unto him, so long as ye both shall live?"

"I do."

Her heart swelled with happiness and love for the man standing next to her, so much so that she scarcely registered the following words spoken by the parson. Mr. Darcy stumbled as he attempted to push a gold ring onto the wrong hand and finger.

Elizabeth thrust her left hand forward, extending her fingers wide apart. He shot her an embarrassed smile, then slid the ring on her fourth finger, the dark blue stone glowing in the morning sunlight streaming through the windows.

She clenched her hand around the weight of the ring and shifted it over to receive the one the parson placed in her palm. It was a big gold ring, obviously used, most likely belonging to Mr. Darcy's father. With a trembling hand, she pushed it onto his left fourth finger.

"I now pronounce you man and wife."

Elizabeth blinked, certain she heard sheep bleating before the congregation erupted into applause. Mr. Darcy shifted towards her, cupping her face in both of his hands. He gazed into her half-lidded eyes, almost like peering into her soul. His head slowly descended towards her lips, their breath mingling before their lips tenderly met. The joy Elizabeth felt was more intense than anything she had ever experienced. She knew she would never forget this moment for as long as she lived.

Mr. Darcy pulled back, a promise in his eyes, then turned to face the congregation with his arm offered for her use, still never taking his sight off her. She intertwined her arm with his and finally faced their friends and relatives.

"Ladies and gentlemen, I present to you, Mr. and Mrs. Darcy."

Mrs. Bennet fluttered her eyes with a handkerchief, Jane's smile beamed, and Mr. Bennet looked stoic, trying to restrain his tears at the loss of his favorite

daughter. Kitty and Mary politely clapped, and the
Gardiners both grinned. Then she scanned Mr.
Darcy's side of the church and nearly burst out
laughing.

Georgiana hopped on her feet, clapping louder than
Mr. Bingley. Mr. Hurst clapped courteously while
Mrs. Hurst leaned to the side, trying to prop up her
sister, who had collapsed.

Her heart brimmed with joy and love as they took
their inaugural steps down the aisle as husband and
wife, arm in arm. They stopped at the first pew
accepting hugs from her sisters, though Jane's was
subdued by a sense of lingering grief. Her anxious
thoughts regarding her sister were cut short by her
mother's handkerchief fluttering in her face before
she was embraced tightly.

Then it was time to hug her father, tears glistening
in both their eyes. Mr. Bennet tried to speak but
failed to utter any words. He nodded to her, shook
Mr. Darcy's hand, and pivoted to escort a tearfully
delighted Mrs. Bennet to the front doors.

Elizabeth trailed her husband's movement and
veered to the left to greet Mr. and Mrs. Hurst. Miss
Bingley exited the pew, nodded, and mumbled

something, still looking nearly as pale as she had at the start of the service.

Then Georgiana dashed out of the pew and hugged her while bouncing joyfully. "I am so blissful!"

She laughed and cheerily reciprocated her new sister's hug. "I am thrilled we are finally sisters!"

Mr. Bingley emerged from the pew last and greeted them both warmly with a hearty handshake for his dear friend. Then he spun to escort Miss Bingley down the aisle and out the church doors. Then the only ones left in the church to greet were the ones responsible for the jubilantly newly married couple being reunited, as the bells of the church chimed.

"Thank you for all you have done. We owe our good luck to you," Mr. Darcy said.

Mr. Gardiner chortled. "Oh, I believe that honor should be accorded to the sheep that catapulted you into the lake."

Mr. Darcy's lips twitched. "I shall have to present it with a bouquet as a token of my thanks."

"He will certainly devour it, perhaps a bunch of carrots instead," Mrs. Gardiner replied.

Elizabeth laughed but was brought short by an auspiciously familiar loud sound from outside the chapel doors: the bleating of sheep! She gasped in confusion. "Sheep?" she exclaimed in bewilderment.

Mr. Darcy and Mr. Gardiner sprinted down the aisle and flung open the church doors. Outside, a flock of sheep had wandered onto the gravel drive and gamboled around cheerfully in circles.

Miss Bingley was screeching, flailing her hands to spook away the bleating mammals that surrounded her on all sides. Georgiana stood on the church steps cackling.

"Good heavens, what is going on here?" exclaimed Mr. Darcy. "Why are there sheep rioting about the churchyard?

Georgiana turned towards her brother. "Of course, the sheep that brought you together would have to be at your wedding!"

Miss Bingley continued to jerk and weep, swinging with her reticule at any ewe that dared encroach upon her person. "Get away from me, you filthy creatures! How dare you surround me in such a manner!"

Mr. Bingley came to his sister's aid, swatting away sheep while escorting her to their carriage. Mr. and Mrs. Hurst quickly followed, expressing disgust and horror at the commotion.

A sheepherder ran towards them, apologizing profusely. "Beg your pardon, Mr. Darcy! They got away from us!"

"Yes. I can see that."

Above the ruckus, standing on the church's front steps, Elizabeth and Mr. Darcy were out of the worst of it. They wisely watched as the sheepherders rounded up the wooly animals and drove them back toward their intended pasture.

"Well!" said Mr. Gardiner.

Mrs. Bennet leaned out of the carriage that presumably held all of the Bennets after they escaped the rampaging sheep. "I have never been so terrified in my life! We had to scramble into our carriage to save our lives!"

Mr. Darcy turned to her with a raised eyebrow, causing Elizabeth to muffle her laughter.

"Thank you all for attending us on this special day. We invite you to the wedding breakfast at Pemberley, where we will celebrate our marriage and spend time together as friends and family."

"Now I know why you barely ate any breakfast!" exclaimed Mr. Bingley standing on the steps of their carriage. "You knew you were going to have a wedding breakfast!" Then he scowled, a look not suited for his perpetually joyous countenance. "Why did you keep this a secret, Darcy?"

He escorted Elizabeth down the steps and towards their carriage as he answered. "To keep my aunt from interfering any further. I am not sure how she continued to be so well-informed."

Georgiana mounted the steps to the Bingley's carriage, the Gardiners clambered into theirs, and the newlywed Darcys finally climbed into their carriage. As Elizabeth reclined against the bench, seated next to Mr. Darcy, she thanked her lucky stars that she had been blessed with such a wonderful man and such an entertaining day already.

As they rolled away from the chapel, Mr. Darcy turned towards her and held her gaze with one steady look. His tender expression revealed admiration and love for her as he leaned in to place a gentle kiss on her lips. His scent was tantalizing, causing her to flush and almost put distance between them on the bench. His thigh was hot against hers until she remembered they were wed, which raised a question.

"I must confess that I am quite curious about how you managed to keep our wedding secret. How did you manage to keep it under wraps for so long?"

He shifted on the bench, looking down with a frown. "I told no one except my senior staff; valet, house-keeper, and cook. They kept it confidential between them."

"Georgiana seemed surprised as well."

Mr. Darcy mischievously grinned. "She sensed something was not right when we passed the Inn. We had planned to call upon you and your sister. Then I informed her the real reason we were in Lambton."

Elizabeth chortled, the subterfuge for a wedding even more amusing since it was her own. "And how did you persuade the unwilling pastor, Mr. Wood-forde, to officiate the wedding? He was very deter-mined to not wed us, particularly not in his church."

He shifted on the bench, looking down with a frown. "I must admit that it was not a pleasant task. But it was made much easier after learning the true reason behind Mr. Woodforde's strong disfavor for the matter."

As Mr. Darcy explained the lengths his aunt went to guarantee her daughter would marry him, Elizabeth's mouth gaped wider. "Goodness, I had no idea that Lady Catherine was capable of such machinations and duplicity. I cannot believe that she would go to such extremes!"

Mr. Darcy nodded in agreement. "Yes, she is more than capable. I am sure we will have to confront her at some point. However, for now, let us revel in our wedding day and all the wonderful memories it will bring."

He paused for a moment and then looked down at her with a tender expression before seizing her lips in a kiss that promised an eternity of bliss between them both.

CHAPTER 24

The sun blazed through the windows at Pemberley, creating a cheerful and inviting atmosphere as the guests gathered in the dining room for the wedding breakfast.

Elizabeth felt a surge of joy course through her as she surveyed the room and beheld all the familiar faces radiating happiness on this momentous occasion. Her husband looked incredibly dashing in his finery, and she could not help but admire him. She blushed when Mr. Darcy caught sight of her watching him. Their eyes locked briefly before they both turned away, unable to suppress the smiles widening on each of their faces.

The clattering of utensils could not drown out Mrs. Bennet's exuberant proclamation. "What incredible luck it is to have a daughter married to someone as distinguished and wealthy as Mr. Darcy! And, of course, that will introduce the girls to other affluent men."

Elizabeth Bennet could not contain the acute embarrassment that coursed through her body at her mother's words. Jane whispered down the table, "Mama!"

Miss Bingley and Mrs. Hurst exchanged a long look while the Gardiners gaped at Mrs. Bennet in varying degrees of shock.

Mr. Bennet merely smiled and said, "Yes indeed...it appears our Elizabeth has found quite the catch."

Mr. Gardiner cleared his throat and rose to salute the newlyweds with a glass of champagne, which was soon followed by raucous cheers from Mr. Bingley and polite applause from the rest.

Throughout the meal, the conversations flowed, and Georgiana grew more vivacious as the morning waned, laughing and talking unreservedly with Elizabeth.

By the end of the breakfast, a feeling of contentment and happiness had taken hold of the room. Guests dispersed to the various rooms in Pemberley, though Caroline excused herself to recline due to an aching head.

Mr. Bingley, Elizabeth was intrigued to notice, had paid close attention to Jane during the breakfast but also seemed agitated. She thought nothing of it until she overheard him asking Mrs. Reynolds if any package had arrived for him from London in the Post.

"No, Mr. Bingley, any packages addressed to you would have been brought to you immediately. I am afraid there has not been any package that has come for you. You say it was posted in London?"

He nodded energetically. "Yes, from my bank." Mr. Bingley ran a hand through his hair. "I had anticipated it to arrive several days ago."

Mrs. Reynolds frowned. "There are difficulties with the Post sometimes, particularly with packages. I am sorry. Could the Postmaster in Lambton provide any assistance?"

Mr. Bingley beamed. "Fantastic! Thank you for the suggestion, Mrs. Reynolds. I shall go there directly!"

Elizabeth grinned to herself, overflowing with the joy of the day and thankful that her mother had not mortified them worse than she already had. Mr. Darcy joined her in the foyer, and they strode into the sitting room arm in arm to the spontaneous applause from Georgiana, with the others quickly following in their wake.

"Where will you go on your wedding trip?" Mrs. Bennet declared with emphatic gestures characteristic of her. "When Mr. Bennet and I went on our trip, we spent three weeks in Brighton near the ocean, and it was a marvelous experience!"

She looked at Mr. Darcy and answered, "It is a wonderful idea, Mama, but I yearn to return to Longbourn to see my friends and to collect my things."

"We can also pass through London along the way," Mr. Darcy added. "Where we can order you a trousseau. It should be ready by our passage through London on our journey home."

Reaching for her hand and clasping it firmly, the room seemed to fade as those hazel eyes transfixed and mesmerized Elizabeth completely.

"Good day, ma'am." Mrs. Reynolds curtsied in reverence as she introduced Elizabeth to the staff of Pemberley. Gesturing towards the doorway, she declared them ready for introduction. Elizabeth thanked her and, accompanied by Mr. Darcy and Georgiana, stepped into the foyer. The servants bowed or curtseyed deferentially to their new mistress of the house. She beamed at each of them, taking note of their various roles and duties.

"It is a pleasure to meet you all," Elizabeth said, feeling a wave of pride and responsibility. She was now the new mistress of such a grand and well-run household. "I trust that we shall work together harmoniously and efficiently to uphold the standards of Pemberley."

"We are honored to serve you, Mrs. Darcy," Mrs. Reynolds spoke on behalf of the staff. "We hope that you will find great joy here."

THE AFTERNOON PASSED QUICKLY, most engaged in pleasantly conversing with friends and family. Mary played the piano in the far corner of the room until

Mr. Bingley entered the sitting room again, his errand to Lambton complete.

Elizabeth greeted his arrival and then studied him intently as he fidgeted, checking a pocket in his coat while repeatedly glancing at her sister Jane. With a spark of hope in her heart, she leaned over to her new husband, whispering an idea.

"Perhaps we could tour the portrait gallery? I have yet to see this beautiful collection with you," she suggested, her eyes meeting his in perfect understanding.

"What an excellent suggestion," Mr. Darcy said warmly with mischievous eyes.

Georgiana leaped to join immediately, and then Jane joined them, expressing her interest. Mr. Bingley quickly followed, and Mr. Darcy ushered them out of the sitting room and into the North Gallery.

As they crossed the threshold, Elizabeth felt a sense of awe wash over her as she took in her surroundings. Every inch of wall space was covered with paintings—portraits of past Darcys.

Mr. Darcy led the way down the long hallway, pointing out specific works.

"Elizabeth," Georgiana said, approaching her from behind. "Which of these is your favorite? There are so many it can be difficult to decide."

Elizabeth glanced around the room and then pointed to one painting in particular.

"I like this one here," she said. "There's something about his expression. He looks so composed and sure of himself yet sympathetic."

Georgiana laughed softly. "That's my favorite, too," she told Elizabeth. "It's our father. He looks so noble and wise. I always feel comforted looking at it."

The two women stood side by side, admiring the portrait in reverent silence. After a pointed look from his wife, Mr. Darcy suggested that Jane might appreciate viewing some of the paintings up ahead. At the same time, he discussed a particular land-scape painting with Elizabeth. With a nervous smile from Mr. Bingley, they moved off together towards an alcove filled with more miniature portraits.

Jane could not help but notice the worried expression on Mr. Bingley's face. "Was your business in Lambton concluded successfully?"

He nervously ran a hand through his hair. "I am afraid not, Miss Bennet," he replied. "You see, I had sent for my mother's ring from the bank vault in London, but it seems the ring has gone missing in the Post."

Jane's heart sank at the news. There was only one reason a man would want his mother's wedding ring. She turned away, willing her tears not to flow.

"I had to purchase a ring in Lambton. I could not wait any longer. I was anxious, well—" Mr. Bingley nervously laughed, then frowned when he noticed Jane was turned away and wiping her face.

"Miss Bennet? Are you unwell?"

"I am well." Jane turned around with a forced smile that quickly fell. "No, I have—"

"—oh good, I have something for you. I mean, I have something to ask you. Oh, dash it all. I am making a mess of this. Will you do me the honor of becoming my wife?"

Jane was dumbfounded. "Your wife?"

"Er, yes." He grew concerned at her expression. "I must apologize for not proposing to you sooner. I had been waiting for my mother's ring to arrive by Post because I wanted you to know how much I love you. Er, Miss Bennet?"

Jane closed the short distance, tears of joy streaming down her face. "Oh, yes. Yes! Yes, I will marry you!"

Mr. Bingley's face beamed joyfully, and he clasped her hands in his. "You have made me the happiest man in the world!"

After producing the ring from his pocket, and with Jane's delighted giggle at his nervousness, the gold ring slid onto her finger, signifying to all that he truly treasured her.

The content couple, intertwined, approached the newlyweds with ecstatic expressions. Mr. Bingley whispered in Jane's ear, then quickly strode towards the library.

"Oh, Lizzy!" She hastened to Elizabeth with a glowing smile, both sisters embracing and guffawing with joy.

"I am so thrilled!" Jane pulled back but retained Elizabeth's hands. Georgiana edged up, standing near

Mr. Darcy. "It is too much. It is too much. Oh, why can't everyone be as merry as I am? He adores me, Lizzy. He adores me!"

"Of course he does." Elizabeth chortled.

"My felicitations," Mr. Darcy stated, echoed by Georgiana.

Jane nodded and then reverted to her sister. "He told me he always loved me, all the time. He didn't trust… I must go and tell Mama." She took a step back and then whirled around. "Oh, he has gone to Papa already. Oh, Lizzy, could you conceive of things concluding in this blissful way?"

"I could, and I do!"

"I must go to Mama." Jane stepped away but then rushed back to Elizabeth, keeping her hands. "Oh, Lizzy…how shall I manage so much joy?"

Then with Elizabeth's cheerful laughter reverberating behind her, Jane darted out of the portrait gallery to find Mrs. Bennet.

The occupants of the sitting room, which now included Caroline Bingley. Miss Bingley reassured the room she was wholeheartedly over her agonizing headache of the morning.

"Mama! I have wonderful news…Mr. Bingley has requested me to marry him," Jane proclaimed jubilantly.

Mrs. Bennet was immediately torn with both surprise and delight—masterfully maneuvering the delicate balance between them. Shedding tears of joy and pride, she stepped forward to enfold her eldest daughter in a loving embrace. Overjoyed at the prospect of seeing her joyfully married off to a man of good fortune, Mrs. Bennet continued to mutter to herself there had always been a reason Jane was so beautiful.

Louisa Hurst stared at Jane Bennet and her mother as they conversed with such exhilaration—perplexity etched all over her features. At the same time, Caroline Bingley kept exchanging looks between them as if trying to make sense of what she had just heard.

Mrs. Gardiner embraced her niece. "It was quite clear that Mr. Bingley was smitten with you. But it was taking so long for him to propose that I feared we would have to get the boisterous sheep involved in the matter and shock some sense into him."

Mr. Gardiner let out a soft chuckle and bestowed Jane a warm embrace. "My dear, you are indeed very blessed—after all, who could reject such a handsome and kind gentleman like Mr. Bingley?"

Jane blushed with her grin. "Thank you, Uncle. I am indeed very fortunate to have won the affections of Mr. Bingley."

"Will we have two balls?" Kitty asked. "One for Lizzy and Mr. Darcy and one for Jane and Mr. Bingley? It would be so thrilling to have two celebrations!"

"Don't be ridiculous!" cried Mrs. Bennet. "The ball we are planning is to celebrate Lizzy's and Jane's weddings, and we must remember to focus on their joy and not get carried away with our own wishes."

Caroline Bingley finally emerged from her stunned state to sneer and share a prolonged disgusted look with Louisa.

Mrs. Bennet continued with her raptures, "The decorations, the food—oh, I simply cannot wait to begin making arrangements! And, of course, new gowns! We shall find the finest fabrics and best fashion trends as we dress you up for such an important affair!"

She wasted no time making plans for the lavish affair, ideas gushing out of her mouth–each spoken with fervor and anticipation.

"Mama, I know you are excited about my engagement to Mr. Bingley, but it is important to remember that the ball we are planning is primarily to celebrate the wedding of Mr. Darcy and Elizabeth. Let's not forget that this is a ball for them, too."

"And it is his house," grumbled Mrs. Hurst with an arched look toward her sister.

Mr. Darcy, Elizabeth, and Georgiana then entered the sitting room after their leisurely stroll from the portrait hall. Mrs. Bennet's voice filled the room as she discussed Jane's upcoming nuptials with her usual grandeur and enthusiasm.

"Jane's wedding will be the grandest event Hertfordshire has ever seen!" Her eyes lit up with excitement as she proclaimed, "We must get her trousseau from London. When I married Mr. Bennet, oh, the gown I had fashioned was something to behold…."

Elizabeth saw Georgiana struggling to hide her laughter, and quickly interjected before her mother could continue. "That's charming, Mama. But maybe we should now go into supper since it is ready?" She gestured to the doorway.

The servant at the doorway bowed and announced that supper was ready to be served.

Mrs. Bennet waved her hand hurriedly. "Of course, of course!"

The Darcys led the procession into the dining room and took their seats at the table. Elizabeth flushed, still amazed that she was the mistress of Pemberley and sitting at Mr. Darcy's right hand.

The growing anticipation of a grand affair filled the air. Already a lively discussion about all the impending details for the ball was underway: what guests would be invited, where they should order their dresses to be ready in time, and, most importantly, what gown should Georgiana wear?

Georgiana's face illuminated in joyous delight at the topic of discussion. After so many years without a grand ball, the prospect of one at Pemberley stirred her with excitement.

As they all enjoyed their supper, Mrs. Bennet continued to regale them with all her thoughts. She spoke nearly unhindered on the decorations, seating arrangements, desserts, and more, much to the annoyance of some and the amusement of others.

Plans were made to visit Lambton the next day to order gowns from the modiste, who had just returned from a trip to London. Hope was alive in the Bennet girls that the modiste would be able to sew their gowns in the latest fashion.

With the great appetites of the guests sated by a well-filled table, a conversation began to stir about what would be occurring in the future for the newly engaged couple.

Mrs. Bennet spoke up enthusiastically, her brown eyes twinkling. "Oh! What a grand time we shall have house hunting for you both! It will be delightful to find just the perfect house fitting for you! Haye Park might do if the Gouldings would vacate it. Or the great house at Stoke if the drawing rooms were larger."

"Or Purvis Lodge," added Kitty.

"Oh, no, dear, not Purvis Lodge." Mrs. Bennet scowled at her daughter. "The attics there are dreadful."

Mr. Darcy shot a questioning glance down the table at Mr. Bingley, whose smile was fading the more his soon-to-be mother-in-law shared her thoughts.

She quickly turned to a new topic, though, of fashion houses in London and who had the best dressmakers available for a trousseau for Jane.

As the meal drew to a close, the women stood in the process of departing the dining room, leaving it to the men for after-dinner drinks and cigars. Mr. Darcy surprised everyone by standing as well.

"It has been a long day, and I am retiring early tonight. But please stay and enjoy yourselves."

Mr. Bingley raised a glass up. "To my good friend, Mr. Darcy, and his wonderful wife, Elizabeth!"

He might have shown something resembling a blush during the applause that broke out. Still, Elizabeth did not honestly know as she was busy fighting her blush and tried not to catch anyone's gaze as she departed the dining room.

Mr. Darcy walked slowly behind her as they ascended the stairs, exchanging small comments about the events of the day until he suddenly swept her into his arms and carried her up to their shared bedroom. Gently setting her down by the open window, letting streams of moonlight touch their faces, they looked out over the Pemberley estate and spoke in whispered tones. Soon lost in each other's presence, Elizabeth nestled her head against Mr. Darcy's chest as they enjoyed their moment together.

The memory of this day would stay with her forever.

CHAPTER 25

The sun shone brightly on the small town, giving it an air of cheerful comfort. The Darcys, along with Mr. Bingley, eager to see his betrothed again, arrived in Lambton with little fanfare. Still, there were a few curious stares from the locals as they descended upon the modiste shop.

Upon entering, they were greeted warmly by the owner, Mrs. Wilson, eager to help them find what they wanted. The Bennet family had already gathered around one of the tables, looking at the various ribbons and lace.

Georgiana stood back, feeling lost in the bewildering crowd of shoppers. Still, Elizabeth helped her new sister-in-law feel at ease.

"What do you think, my dear?" Mr. Darcy asked Elizabeth as he surveyed the store. His voice was low and gentle, his eyes locked on hers.

Elizabeth smiled. "I think it's perfect. The selection is greater than I had expected. The colors are so vivid and the fabrics so luxurious."

Just then, Mrs. Bennet burst into the conversation. "Oh, just look at all these lovely laces and ribbons! It is enough to make me swoon! We must get some for each of my girls!"

Everyone in the shop suddenly grew silent while Elizabeth and Jane shared a long look, used to their mother's foibles.

Mr. Bingley quickly regained his composure and cleared his throat. "Yes, well...I am sure they will look quite splendid."

They wandered through the store, inspecting the different notions and discussing the alterations they would need to make to the gowns to prepare them for the ball. As they did, news of their marriage rapidly spread throughout the town. People stopped to whisper and gape, peering through the shop's windows.

Their alterations finalized, the large group left the shop, to the well-wishes of the townsfolk gathered outside. Elizabeth blushed at the attention. She had not anticipated this from marrying Mr. Darcy. He was not nobility, but his ten thousand per annum brought the same regard in his home county. She smiled and thanked the townspeople for their kindness as she glanced at her husband, her heart overflowing.

The group then set forth for Pemberley, the Bennets, with their baggage in tow as they took up residence at the estate until after the ball. The journey was pleasant as they talked of their enthusiasm for the coming ball. Georgiana was particularly delighted, as this would be her first ball and the only one she could recall being held at Pemberley.

As they approached the estate, Elizabeth was overcome again with amazement by the stunning view that unfolded before her. She had only visited Pemberley a few weeks prior, yet it felt like she was seeing it for the first time again. The lake glimmered in the sunlight, the ducks and geese floating peacefully atop its surface. At the same time, the gardens brimmed with vibrant colors and aromas. It was as if a masterpiece of nature had been painted across the landscape.

She glanced at Mr. Darcy from the corner of her eye and found him looking back at her with a soft smile. Her heart swelled with joy, astonished that she had been blessed enough to marry for love. He squeezed her hand gently, and she returned the gesture, feeling a warmth deep within her.

The carriages pulled up to the main house, and the Bennets and Gardiners alighted with pleasure. They had all accepted Mr. Darcy's invitation to stay at Pemberley and couldn't wait to explore the estate and make use of all it had to offer. The Gardiners' carriage arrived shortly after the others.

Mrs. Bennet's exuberance was evident as she stepped out of the carriage. "Oh, what a dream come true! To think that my girls will be living at Pemberley and taking advantage of all its features! How wonderful!"

Mr. Darcy shared a meaningful glance with Mr. Bingley, who responded with a nervous chuckle. Elizabeth braced herself for her mother's complete lack of propriety until her family left Pemberley following the ball.

As they all entered Pemberley, Caroline Bingley's stiff smile and Louisa Hurst's pinched lips turned into a grimace of horror as they realized the Bennet family was moving into the guest wing.

After a hasty luncheon, Georgiana and Elizabeth worked together with the housekeeper to perfect the arrangements for the ball the ensuing day. They chose the menu, a combination of opulent and elegant dishes from both English and French cuisine. The housekeeper assured them that only the finest ingredients would be purchased from the local markets, beginning at dawn the next day.

The entire house bustled with energy and life as servants hurried about in anticipation of the ball tomorrow night. As darkness descended on Pemberley, excitement built. They all gathered for supper and spent the evening together with games and conversation. Kitty expressed her hope to dance every set. Georgiana played the harp before all retired to their chambers for the night.

The night passed swiftly, and soon enough, the long-awaited day of the ball had arrived. The day was spent in busy preparation, with Mrs. Wilson and her assistants ensuring the Bennet sisters' gowns fit them perfectly. Elizabeth couldn't help but feel anxious as she dressed in her beautiful gown. She glanced in the mirror one last time.

Mr. Darcy took Elizabeth's hands in his and looked into her eyes. He softly stroked her knuckles with his thumb, sending a warmth coursing through her body that settled deep in her chest.

"I know not why I have been so fortunate as to gain your hand in marriage, but I give thanks to Providence daily," he uttered softly.

Elizabeth felt the tears well up in her eyes as she looked into his warm brown ones. She laughed softly. "It is hard to believe we have come so far. It only seems like yesterday we were strangers."

"We certainly are not strangers anymore," Mr. Darcy said with a smile.

He leaned in and kissed her tenderly before pulling away and brushing his nose against hers.

"Let's go down and join the guests at the ball," he said as he tucked a strand of hair behind her ear.

With a contented sigh, Elizabeth nodded and smiled, taking his arm as they strode from their chambers and descended the stairs. Standing alongside Mr. Darcy and Georgiana, Elizabeth greeted the guests as they arrived. She was aware that a few guests were curiously eyeing her as if speculating whether she could genuinely be Mrs. Darcy. A slight blush arose as she introduced herself to the arriving guests, smiling politely. Mr. Darcy, meanwhile, stood tall and proud as he welcomed the guests to Pemberley. His gaze never wandered far from Elizabeth, a silent promise of love and protection in his eyes. Georgiana smiled warmly at the guests, her beauty captivating them all.

When it was time for the ball to begin, Mr. Darcy offered Elizabeth his arm. "Shall we?"

Elizabeth smiled and accepted his arm as they marched up the stairs. As soon as they stepped into the ballroom, Georgiana excitedly exclaimed, "Oh, what a stunning sight!"

The ballroom at Pemberley was a sight to behold. Artfully arranged floral arrangements, sparkling chandeliers, and elegant drapery decorated the walls. The plaster was freshly painted in a soft ivory color that complemented the delicate pastels of the gowns worn by the attendees. Glassware glittered from the tables, and the soft glow from the candles created a romantic atmosphere.

The orchestra began to play a waltz, and Mr. Darcy extended his hand to Elizabeth. She could feel her heart pounding as they stepped onto the dance floor to begin the first dance of the evening. They spun around each other gracefully, making the most intricate and elegant patterns with the musicians playing an upbeat tune.

Soon the entire ballroom was filled with laughter and conversation. Everyone looked their best in their finery, and the music soared above them as couples whirled around the floor.

As they twisted their way around the room, Elizabeth greeted many familiar faces from Lambton. She endeavored to make conversation with everyone she encountered. Mr. Darcy stood with pride beside her. Together they welcomed their guests and many of the illustrious society members that had come to celebrate their union.

Mrs. Bennet couldn't help but be pleased that her unmarried daughters had the opportunity to meet so many eligible, wealthy suitors this evening. "It is wonderful to see them enjoying themselves and having such a splendid time," she said with a contented sigh. "I sincerely hope some of these handsome young men will soon make an offer for one of my daughters. Of course, none of them measure up to Jane, but surely Kitty and Mary will do their best."

Mr. Darcy and Elizabeth exchanged an awkward glance while Georgiana averted her gaze, her cheeks turning pink in embarrassment. Elizabeth ignored her mother's comments and focused on the joyous occasion. She and Mr. Darcy had opened the ball and danced nearly every set since but were now taking a much-needed respite.

Her happiness continued to blossom as she watched her family and friends enjoy themselves. Radiant in her pink gown, Jane laughed merrily as she twirled in Mr. Bingley's arms. She smiled radiantly at her dearest sister, filled with joy, knowing that Jane would soon be wed to the man that had captured her heart so long ago.

The laughter and conversation that filled the hall only added to the atmosphere of pure delight. It was clear that all eyes were upon the happy couple as they moved gracefully around the floor. Elizabeth smiled fondly at their guests before striding to the center of the room for the next set. As they began to dance, she felt the warmth of his touch and the love that surrounded them, and she knew that this night would genuinely be one they'd never forget.

After the dance set had finished, they had barely left the dance floor before they noticed a commotion by the doorway. A loud, shrill voice could be heard coming from the stairs and reverberating throughout the ballroom. Immediately, the guests began to whisper and speculate about who was causing the uproar.

As they glanced at each other in confusion and hastened towards the mezzanine, Elizabeth realized with dawning horror that she recognized the source of the commotion.

"You must let me through! Do you know who I am?" The voice grew ever louder. "My nephew has no right to host this ball to celebrate his engagement with that Bennet girl!"

The shock at Lady Catherine's outburst was palpable throughout the ballroom, causing many guests to gasp audibly in surprise.

Mr. Darcy stepped forward, his face a mask of determination. "Lady Catherine," he said firmly. "I am afraid there is nothing to be done. Elizabeth and I are no longer engaged. We are married."

At this announcement, Lady Catherine's face turned an alarming shade of purple as every eye in the ballroom was riveted upon her. She gaped at the couple, her mouth opening and closing in disbelief.

Then she stilled, her gaze focused on someone behind Elizabeth, her ladyship's eyes nearly bulging as she raised her arm and pointed. "It is your fault! You were supposed to keep me informed!"

The crowd around them had gone deathly silent as they watched the drama unfold. All eyes turned towards Caroline, who seemed to pale under the intensity of Lady Catherine's glare.

Footmen rushed to Lady Catherine's side, trying to help her out of the ballroom as she shouted about the "shades of Pemberley" being polluted by such a union. Many guests were taken aback by her outburst, some even snickering under their breaths.

By this time, Mr. Darcy had signaled the musicians who had started playing again, and couples began to flock to the dance floor once more. Though the atmosphere was now slightly awkward, people seemed determined to enjoy themselves and make the best of the situation. Everyone continued to steal glances towards the doorway where Lady Catherine de Bourgh had recently departed with the help of several footmen.

Elizabeth felt relieved that the situation had been diffused so quickly. Still, she also felt a slight twinge of sadness, knowing that Lady Catherine would never accept her into the family. She glanced up at Mr. Darcy, grateful for his unwavering support during this challenging moment. He squeezed her hand gently in reassurance.

As they watched the festivities continue, Elizabeth thought about how the evening could have gone differently. Still, she was determined to make the most of their special day. She smiled at Mr. Darcy, and together they took their place among the other guests, determined to revel in the rest of the night.

The remainder of the night was a flurry of activity and excitement as the guests continued to mingle and dance. All except for Caroline Bingley, who had quickly fled the ballroom along with her sister after Lady Catherine's shocking accusation. Mr. Darcy had wanted to throw her out immediately, but Elizabeth tempered his ire to wait until the morning.

As the hour grew late, many of the guests began to take their leave. The newlyweds stood at the entrance of Pemberley, bidding their guests farewell with a gracious nod or smile. As the last carriages pulled away, the couple breathed a sigh of relief. They turned to each other, both suddenly aware of the exhaustion that had settled over them.

Elizabeth glanced up at Mr. Darcy, who smiled at her affectionately, and giggled. "I think we should thank those sheep," she said, her gaze twinkling mischievously.

Mr. Darcy chuckled, shaking his head in amusement. "Indeed we should," he said, leaning down to brush a light kiss against her forehead.

They strolled up the stairs, their steps echoing in the stillness of the night. As they reached the top of the stairs, Elizabeth paused, turning to look back at the empty ballroom to the left.

She could still feel the energy of the night lingering in the air. "It was a most successful evening, don't you think?" she asked, a small smile playing on her lips.

Mr. Darcy nodded, the corner of his mouth twitching with amusement. "Indeed it was. I can safely say that all our guests left with something to talk about."

Elizabeth laughed. The shades of Pemberley had never been so alive.

EPILOGUE

Several months after the Pemberley Ball, Mr. Darcy and Elizabeth were just as happy as ever. They departed their home in Derbyshire to visit another pair that had also recently wed: Mr. Bingley and Jane Bennet. The newlyweds were established at Netherfield Hall and had invited the Darcys for the winter holidays.

As the Darcy carriage approached the manor house, Elizabeth turned and beamed at her husband. Mr. Darcy matched her gaze with a small smile. "Do you remember my stay at Netherfield to care for my ill sister?"

"How could I possibly forget? It was when I realized I was in danger of falling in love with you."

Elizabeth giggled. "You were in danger of me? Of my strong opinions?"

Mr. Darcy's lips twitched. "Indeed not. I was terrified of your mother."

Elizabeth laughed, tossing her head back, and Georgiana gasped next to them.

Elizabeth opened her eyes, still chuckling, to find her husband staring at her with such deep affection. Georgiana chose that moment to interject. "Brother, how can you...but you are not frightened of anything?"

Mr. Darcy regretfully reined in his desire for his wife and addressed his sister. "Mrs. Bennet...is best experienced in small doses."

Elizabeth tore her gaze from her handsome husband to take in Georgiana's shocked face. "It is not idle gossip. I know well my mother's proclivities to be dramatic. She can be a bit excessive to handle. Even on the best of days."

They ceased the conversation to turn to look at the grand estate as their carriage pulled in front of Netherfield Hall and halted. How long ago Mr. Bingley had last resided here, and much had transpired. It would be a delightful Christmastime for both couples.

Jane dashed down the hall with her arms open, eager to greet her sister.

"Oh wait, let me remove my wrappings first, Jane!"

Jane did not let that stop her and embraced Elizabeth in a tight embrace while her husband clasped hands with his best friend. "Darcy! You made an excellently timed arrival! Any troubles on the road?"

"None at all. It was a pleasant journey."

The servants took the travelers' winter outerwear, and the Darcys were ushered into the dining room for hot drinks and a meal. Every surface was adorned exquisitely with holly and mistletoe, and the scene of pine cones permeated the air. Everywhere she looked, beautiful baubles and ornaments hung from the chandelier.

"Oh, Jane," Elizabeth breathed. "It looks so wonderful!"

Mr. Darcy smiled, looking just as pleased as his wife. "It certainly does," he concurred. "You have done an impressive job."

"We thought it might be a nice change to brighten the house for Christmas," Jane said, smiling as she looked around the room. "Charles has been very busy with many improvements to Netherfield Hall, and we wanted to do something special for the holidays."

Mr. Bingley nodded in agreement. "Indeed. I thought it would be nice to plan something for the whole neighborhood. We thought that a small Christmas gathering would just get us all in the spirit!" He explained their plans, his enthusiasm growing with each word. "We begin with a dinner party here at Netherfield."

Mr. Darcy, not one for gatherings with people he did not know well, seemed resigned to the inevitability of such an event. "I am sure everyone will enjoy themselves immensely."

Mr. Bingley beamed at the compliment. "Thank you, Darcy. It's been a pleasure to plan it all out with the help of Mrs. Bingley," Charles said, taking a moment to reach out for Jane's hand as she blushed.

THE DARCYS RETIRED TO BED, exhausted from the several days of travel. Elizabeth moved to the bed and began to disrobe, her husband's gaze upon her as he advanced to stand beside her. She felt his warmth and inhaled his scent, a profound sense of contentment settling over her as she prepared for the night.

He extended his hand and caressed her arm lightly, his eyes full of love. "It's our first Christmas together," he murmured softly.

Elizabeth smiled, reaching up to brush his cheek. "Yes. Christmas is my favorite time of year." Mr. Darcy leaned in to chastely kiss her forehead, then stepped back and began to undress. After they finished and settled into bed, Elizabeth reached out and entwined her fingers with his.

"We should tell your family soon," he said, gazing into her eyes. "I am sure they will be elated."

Elizabeth nodded, though she could not help feeling a little apprehensive. "And Georgiana too," she added, biting her lip. "She is going to adore being an aunt."

Mr. Darcy smiled and squeezed her hand gently. "Yes, she will. But do not worry. We can wait till after Christmas. Even Epiphany if you want."

Elizabeth nodded and snuggled closer to her husband. "I do not want to keep the news a secret when I know how ecstatic it will make everyone. But I do not want to share it too soon either."

Mr. Darcy pressed a tender kiss to her forehead.

THE NEXT DAY, with the final preparations for the dinner party complete, all returned to their rooms to dress for the party. The young women exchanged smiles as they examined each other's ensembles, all wearing gowns trimmed with red, white, green, or gold in honor of the holiday.

As the sun set, carriages began to arrive, bringing the Bennet family and their neighbors, the Lucas family.

"Mama! Papa! I am so glad you could make it," Jane said as she hugged each of them.

"Oh, la! It was but two miles, not a nearly a hardship!" Mrs. Bennet exclaimed, perfectly content with how close her eldest daughter lived and how far her second eldest daughter lived.

After all the guests arrived, the group moved into the dining hall for supper, with the Lucas family being the last to arrive. As they took their seats, Jane's careful planning was evident. The tables had been exquisitely set with fine china and crystal glasses, and the food smelled divine. Everyone complimented Jane on her hostess skills, and soon the meal began.

The conversation was lively, with each person sharing stories from past Christmases or funny anecdotes from recent experiences. Everyone was in high spirits, especially Mr. and Mrs. Bennet, who were delighted to be celebrating the holidays with their entire family again, except their youngest, who was still far north with her husband. Mrs. Bennet had already complained at least three times about her poor Lydia not having enough funds to travel to Hertfordshire. She looked pointedly at both her sons by marriage.

Suddenly, Kitty Bennet spoke up, her voice inquisitive. "Where is Miss Caroline Bingley? I haven't seen her yet."

Mr. Bingley sighed, his face turning a bit pink. "Ah, yes. She is in London with our sister Hurst."

"She is still quite determined to find a husband, then? I wish her all the luck. She will certainly need it at her age," cried Mrs. Bennet.

Embarrassed glances were exchanged, but Sir William Lucas, ever the gentleman, introduced a topic of conversation that sparked hearty discussion.

Elizabeth suppressed her amusement as she glanced at Mr. Darcy, who gave her a small smile back. Everyone present knew that Caroline had been banned from Mr. Darcy's presence after her behavior while staying at Pemberley earlier that year. As for his aunt, she was also not welcome, especially not after she had sent several missives that were so abusive they were used to fuel the fire in Mr. Darcy's study.

As the second course began, the group was presented with an array of desserts. From creamy custards to decadent chocolate cakes, there was something for everyone. As everyone indulged in the decadent treats, the conversation became more lighthearted and laughter filled the room.

When dinner had been finished, the guests moved back into the sitting room, and caroling was proposed. It quickly became one of the highlights of the evening. The harmonizing voices filled the hall with Christmas cheer, and the laughter that followed amplified it. Mr. Darcy took the lead on many of them as his baritone voice resonated through the room.

Elizabeth sang along with her husband, her sweet soprano echoing through the hall. Mary sang harmoniously with her sister Kitty, while Georgiana's delicate tones blended harmoniously with Mrs. Bennet's alto. The Lucas family chimed in enthusiastically, joining perfectly with the others.

The music filled the air with joy, and soon everyone sang at full volume. Even those who weren't particularly gifted at singing sang loudly, relishing in the festive atmosphere. As the carol's last notes faded, laughter reverberated through the hall.

Sir William Lucas exclaimed, "What a beautiful evening this has been! There is nothing quite like joyful singing to bring Christmas cheer! I am so pleased to have been a part of this wonderful gathering. Thank you, Mr. and Mrs. Bingley, for your wonderful hospitality!"

The evening concluded in merriment and contentment. The Bennet family was the last to leave. As their carriage drove away, they looked back at Netherfield in admiration.

Mrs. Bennet gushed with enthusiasm, "Oh, what a wonderful evening! I must say, the Bingleys have outdone themselves! The food was delectable, and the decorations were exquisite.

Mary interjected, "I thought the conversation was quite stimulating. I enjoyed the discussion on the economy of the current times."

Kitty chimed in, "And the singing was so much fun! I loved it when Mr. Darcy led a carol. His voice was so beautiful."

"I daresay the Lucas' would never find such a fine table at the Collins." Mrs. Bennet glanced out the window, "Ah, we are nearly home. And what a perfect way to end our evening."

"It was good to see them, especially Lizzy," said Mr. Bennet, gazing forlornly out the window.

It was Christmas morning in the English countryside, and all were venturing to church. The winter air was crisp, and the scenery around them was peaceful and breathtaking. An entrancing blanket of snow lay across the rolling hills.

As soon as the group from Netherfield arrived at the church, they could feel the warmth and joy radiating from the walls. The tall stained-glass windows cast an ethereal light throughout the room. The sermon was filled with hope and joy, focusing on Christmas's true meaning and the importance of family.

As the parson spoke, Elizabeth and Mr. Darcy exchanged knowing glances and warm smiles. Jane and Mr. Bingley sat close together, exchanging sweet comments with each other. Georgiana listened intently, her heart overflowing with gratitude for the blessings she had received that day.

As the group arrived at Longbourn, they were greeted by the delightful smells of Christmas dinner and the cheerful laughter of the Bennet family. Everyone quickly gathered around the fire, eager to begin opening their gifts.

Mrs. Bennet began by handing out a small parcel to each person. As each opened their present, they exclaimed with delight at the thoughtful gifts inside. Jane received a beautiful pair of gloves, while Mary was presented with a new book. Georgiana was delighted with a new necklace from Mr. Darcy and Elizabeth and Kitty with a new gown.

When it came time for Mr. Darcy and Elizabeth to present their gifts, everyone's attention was focused on them. With a beaming smile, Elizabeth accepted the box from Mr. Darcy and opened it to find a stunning emerald necklace. Tears of joy streamed down her face as she held it up to the light, and murmurs of admiration spread throughout the room.

Mrs. Bennet, her eyes glittering with emotion, clasped her hands together and exclaimed, "Oh, Lizzy, it is simply beautiful! Such a thoughtful gift from your beloved husband!"

Elizabeth blushed under the praise and smiled in gratitude at her husband. She replied, "Thank you, Fitzwilliam."

Mr. Darcy nodded, his eyes twinkling with pleasure. "It is my pleasure. I am delighted that you approve of my choice."

Mr. Bingley then presented Jane with a small, leather-bound box. She opened it to find a beautiful gold bracelet with a single sapphire. Jane gasped with delight and exclaimed, "Oh, Charles! It is so beautiful!"

Mr. Bingley smiled, his eyes twinkling with joy. "I am glad. I was not sure which gem to purchase, but the blue goes so well with your eyes, I had to have it!"

Kitty chimed in, "It is almost as beautiful as the necklace Mr. Darcy gave Elizabeth!"

Mary gazed at her sister with censure. "You can hardly compare the two gifts. Each is so special in its own way and very thoughtful of the giver."

Mr. Bennet nodded. "Indeed, it is a very thoughtful gift."

Jane smiled at her husband, her eyes sparkling with happiness. "Thank you, Charles. It is perfect." She kissed him lightly on the cheek before returning to her seat.

After all the presents had been opened, the group settled down to enjoy the wonderful feast that had been prepared. As they ate and drank, the conversation flowed freely, each person recounting their favorite moments from the day. Finally, when everyone was full and content, the group retired to the drawing room for tea and conversation.

Suddenly, Mr. Darcy cleared his throat and announced, "We have something else we would like to share. Elizabeth is expecting our first child."

The room fell silent as everyone processed the news. Finally, Mrs. Bennet burst into tears of joy and embraced both of them tightly.

Mr. Bingley was the first to speak, clapping his hands in delight. "This is wonderful news! Congratulations, Darcy and Elizabeth!"

Jane beamed, her eyes shining with joy. "Oh, Lizzy! I am so happy for you!" She hugged her sister tightly, tears streaming down her face.

Kitty and Mary jumped up from their seats and exclaimed congratulations, their faces bright with excitement.

Mrs. Bennet wiped her eyes and said, "My dear, I can hardly believe it. You are going to be parents! I am so very pleased for both of you."

Mr. Bennet stepped forward, his expression one of pride. "I couldn't be happier for you both."

Georgiana smiled, her eyes misting with tears. "I am so excited to be an aunt! I can't wait to meet the baby."

Elizabeth and Mr. Darcy shared a loving glance, their hearts filled with joy. This Christmas was one that none of them would ever forget.

The rest of the day was spent celebrating the happy announcement and preparing for the feast ahead. Mr. Darcy and Elizabeth left that evening with full hearts, knowing that this was only the beginning of a beautiful future together.

The End

Thank you for reading! View Bella Breen's catalog of books.

For my steamy Mr. Darcy and Elizabeth stories view my Demi Monde books.

If you would like to know when I release a new book, and have a secret sale just for my newsletter subscribers, sign up for my newsletter. Yes, please, sign me up!

If you enjoyed the story I hope you'll consider leaving a review. Reviews are vital to any author's career, and I would be extremely thankful and appreciative if you'd consider writing one for me.

Made in the USA
Monee, IL
07 January 2023

24790435R00184